A MARRIAGE WELL DONE

BOO WALKER

SANDY
—PRESS—
RUN

ALSO BY BOO WALKER

Red Mountain

Red Mountain Rising

Red Mountain Burning

An Unfinished Story

The Singing Trees

A Spanish Sunrise

Writing as Benjamin Blackmore:

Lowcountry Punch

Once a Soldier

Off You Go: A Mystery Novella

For Debbie Ice and Nina Krammer,
two sorceresses of language

A MARRIAGE WELL DONE

Boo Walker

1

THE PRESSURE COOKER

On a frigid December day in Burlington, Vermont, as the anger of a crumbling marriage filled every part of me, I sprinkled a white powder into my husband's Scotch and gave the concoction a quick stir. Seeing the powder dissolve into the brown liquid made me feel like someone was covering me with a warm blanket on that cold, lifeless day.

No, I wasn't going to kill him. Not yet, anyway. Believe it or not, I was acting from a place of love and only wanted to see him squirm as a few hives and rashes rose on his skin—a mild allergic reaction. Assuming I'd chosen the correct dosage—or, overdosage in this case—I'd find enough satisfaction in his discomfort to keep faking my smiles for another day or two.

Through the window, past the strings of Christmas lights lining the back-porch railing, I could see snow falling onto our vast lawn that stretched to the forest, reminding me of our first snowfall after having moved to this house almost two decades ago. As I wrapped my fingers around his tainted drink, I could almost see our younger selves throwing snowballs back and forth, laughing like only newlyweds could. Those two lovers had no idea what lay ahead.

Glass in hand, I went to find my husband. He'd driven me to this point, and I'd run out of options. Waltzing down the hall like a mad Mary Poppins, I sang, "A spoonful of sugar makes the medicine go down, the medicine go down, the medicine go down."

~

ALLOW me to back up for a moment, and please—despite how ugly it might get—try not to pass judgment until you've heard the entire story.

When my husband lost his way, stopped "seeing" me, and our marriage inevitably decayed, I decided I would do everything in my power to get him back. Divorce was not an option. Where I come from, you figure out how to make it work. You don't run for cover the moment it rains. You take your partner's hand and dance in the downpour. Besides, I was Margot, the Hallmark-Channel-and-*Under-the-Tuscan-Sun*-watching dreamer, a woman who refused to believe that I had chosen the wrong husband or that my heart had led me astray.

That's why for nearly a year, I'd been executing a ludicrous New Year's resolution to make my husband love me again and to save my marriage. Looking back, I suppose I went about things differently from most of the invisible wives out there, and I now see the error of my ways. Rather than pointing out our marital issues and asking (forcing) my husband to go to couple's therapy with me, I thought it might be a good idea to improve myself, or "raise my game," as my husband would say, pulling from his deep bag of hockey lingo. I lacked self-confidence and struggled with self-doubt. Maybe it was I who was causing the problems. Maybe I wasn't worth being loved anymore.

So I did everything I could to become Superwife. I needed to give exactly what I wanted to receive in a marriage. If I led by example, I could show him how to love me again. I would be a bright light in the dark tunnel he'd lost himself in—even if that meant becoming a figurative punching bag and a shell of the woman I used to be.

The main issue, as you'll discover, was that my definition of the best *me* was all wrong. With each day, I had moved further away from my true self. Revisiting the memories now, nothing about my plan made sense. What did changing *me* have to do with changing *him* at all? We were destined to walk a rocky road. Ah, the 20/20 of hindsight. When you lose yourself to please someone else, no one comes out unscathed.

There was a devious twist to this project of becoming Superwife. I couldn't let him have all the fun. If I committed to working hard to strengthen emotionally, change physically, and succumb to every one of his demands, I expected a little something in return. It wouldn't be easy to transform myself while also doing my best not to point out his flaws—he wasn't exactly easy to live with—so I created a solution to deal with the certain fury that, at times, would surely bubble up inside me. At times, I felt like a nuclear meltdown waiting to happen.

I likened this solution to turning the release valve on one of my favorite tools in the kitchen, the pressure cooker, which was quickly regaining popularity in the United States. While I bent over backward for this man, even when he ignored, insulted, or just plain annoyed me, I would feel a pressure building that would require release before an explosion occurred. In fact, I'd already tested this pressure-cooker idea, and I'd been correct in my hypothesis. The occasional release allowed me to forge ahead with the plan of being the (almost) perfect wife.

If you're not familiar with a pressure cooker, let me brief you. I consider my cooking life broken into two parts. Before I discovered this amazing invention, and after. I use it nearly every day. I can cook beans, rice, quinoa, soups, hard-boiled eggs, and a thousand other things so easily and quickly. When the food's ready, you turn the release valve and a tremendous amount of steam spits out, almost like that from a steam engine's cylinders while racing down the line. From my newfound, healthier vantage point, it was abundantly clear that my own train was about to veer off its tracks.

What could I have done to turn the valve and release the steam on my emotional pressure cooker, you ask? I think this is the part you'll find most entertaining about my story. It is as sad as can be, but I can now laugh at the absurdity. Let's say, with a little creativity, I could exact revenge on my husband without his even knowing it! His ignorance was the key to my plan's success. I certainly could not make him fall in love with me again if he knew I was anything less than perfect. No, this plan required a stealthy Margot Simpson to appear flawless in every way. To be the woman of my husband's dreams. Only in the background, slyly, deviously, and expertly, could I wage my subtle revenge, hence turning my release valve.

I became the queen of the passive-aggressive onslaught.

Back when dinosaurs roamed the earth, when I was young and full of energy and barely into my twenties, I was working on and off Broadway, doing exactly what I'd wanted to do since I was a little girl. Gosh, from as far back as I can remember, I'd been an entertainer. I'd grown from a little girl singing songs with my mother, to performing for family and friends in our living room, to grabbing the lead in plays throughout grade school. In college, I'd double-majored in music and drama. Then, as stage actors who crave the ultimate success in their profession do, I'd moved to New York City. Within months, I'd nabbed a role in my first off-Broadway show.

By the time my husband found me, I was performing a three-month run playing Polly in a re-run of *Crazy for You*. Our production was coming to an end when I first spotted him in the crowd, and by then, we owned the stage. I'd never had so much fun working with a cast and crew before. That night, when we came out for the final bow, a man in the audience and I locked eyes for a moment. I remember the lightness I felt in my heart. It was almost as if, during our brief eye contact, he'd put me on his back and flown me into the air like a bird. He returned several more times, and each time he sat closer and closer to the stage. As it was a sold-out show, I could hardly believe he had not only found tickets, but good tickets at that. Who was this man?

On the fourth night of his attendance, I found a bouquet of lilies and a note waiting for me backstage. My heart leapt as I read his wonderful comments about my performance. His name was Rory Simpson. To my disappointment, he hadn't left his number, but on the night of our last show, after our final bow, I strutted to the end of the stage, thanked him for the flowers, and we shook hands. A lightning bolt of energy surged through me as he boldly kissed my cheek. The next day, we met for coffee and meandered through Central Park. Rory was leaving the next morning, so he persuaded me to have dinner with him that night. After a lovely candlelit meal in an Italian restaurant on the Upper West Side, we kissed, and I fell under his spell. He proposed six months later in Central Park, and I left my Broadway career to become a homemaker in Vermont.

I never resented the move. The choice hadn't been difficult.

I had finally found the life I'd been singing about for years. I happily walked away from my stage career because, more than success in that arena, I wanted a family. Fighting for new roles would become increasingly difficult as I grew older, but my roles as a wife and a mother would be permanent. I craved permanence. Blowing the minds of my family and friends, I married Rory Simpson and became a Vermonter. A few years later, I gave birth to our son Jasper, who grew to be a kind and gentle boy who didn't deserve the suffering that would come his way.

It's important that I don't paint an unfair picture of Rory. He is a good man deep down. For a very long time, he had been a great husband and father. It's just that his career trajectory hadn't left much room for family. Rory eventually ran for mayor of Burlington and won. I remember feeling extremely happy and proud, but I had no idea how much his new job would consume him. Toward the end of his first four years, when he started to talk about running for the senate, he checked out of our family. Point being, if I get carried away in the developing story and let some of my anger toward him surface, please remember that he had been my dream man for many years.

Things got in the way. Isn't that what often happens?

In addition to having been a chaser of fairy tales, I must admit that I also had been afraid of being alone. That's easier to see now. After you've spent twenty years with someone, you can't imagine saying goodbye. No matter who he becomes or what he does or says, he's a part of you. Go find a couple that has gone through a miserable divorce, and I bet they will confess—possibly under extreme torture—that they're still connected. Not only was it nearly impossible for me to imagine trudging through the rest of life without a partner, I also couldn't imagine fighting over custody of our son. How could we possibly do that to Jasper? I would happily sacrifice my happiness to give him a secure childhood in a two-parent home.

It was the second week of December when I noticed my plan was backfiring. It had begun as a New Year's resolution in January. Almost one year in, and I was unraveling. But I told myself that often the struggle becomes strongest when you're close to winning. I couldn't give up at that point. My parents were still together, and I wanted to celebrate the same longevity with my husband. I had spent the entire year doing everything I could to turn our relationship around, including losing weight, cutting my hair, letting Rory do whatever he pleased, and loving him when he didn't respond with even an iota of love back. How could I have stopped mid-plan? I believed if I kept trudging through, he'd wake up and realize what he had—what we had.

Back to the mad Mary Poppins story, only an hour before I sprinkled the powder into Rory's drink. It was Christmastime in Vermont, and I was singing a much different song. I was high on the Christmas spirit, singing "Deck the Halls," and easing down our long paved driveway that wound through a forest of tall snow-covered evergreens. I'd left to pick up several extra bags of ice for the party we were hosting that night, but I wasn't worried about the ice melting on the way back. I was in no hurry. The holidays were my favorite time of year, and I did everything I could to slow down the moments. As I passed the last trees of the forest, our century-old white Victorian home with a wraparound porch came into view, standing proudly in the middle of several acres of snow. The array of lights and decorations on and around the house brought vibrant reds and greens to the all-encompassing winter white.

Many people decorate for Christmas around Thanksgiving

time. That seems to be the American rule. I cheat and string lights on the Friday before Halloween (yes, you read that right!), and by Thanksgiving our house and property were so covered in Christmas decorations that we could have charged money for people to visit. I think I jumped into my role as a home-maker like I dove into my past acting roles, giving it everything I had. Lights and topiaries hung from the lampposts that lined the last part of the driveway. Rory had let me get away with putting a life-size sleigh, Santa, and all his reindeer on the lawn near our front porch. I waved at Santa.

Parking next to my husband's Cadillac by the side of the house, I stacked up the bags of ice in the snow and planned to return later to retrieve them. I typically enter through the side door, but on that day, I wanted to make sure the front remained neat for the company arriving later. I climbed the front steps and admired my handiwork. One of the most beautiful wreaths on planet Earth adorned our red front door. Through a window to the left, I could see the largest of our five Christmas trees twinkling by the fireplace in the living room. I pushed open the door and was greeted by Bing Crosby's jolly voice. There were rules in my house during the holidays. Only Christmas music was allowed. We were a festive bunch. By "we," I mean "*I*" in particular.

Most Decembers, I had the pleasure of entering our home to hear Jasper playing a holiday tune on his grand piano in the living room. But our teenage son was attending a winter music camp through a school exchange program. I'd like to claim credit for some of his musical virtuosity, but his piano talents extended far beyond my ability. Yes, I had majored in music, and I had made a career at it before I'd met Rory, but I had only a fraction of Jasper's musical ability. Before he'd even turned ten years old, he was tearing through Liszt, Chopin, and Rachmaninoff, and had won every competition he'd entered. We knew scholarships were in his future and that we wouldn't be paying for college. As long as Rory and I—and our mess— stayed out of the way, Jasper would achieve any piano dream he could imagine.

Philippe, my young terrier mutt, heard the door close. First, I heard him barking, and he soon came barreling clumsily around the corner, slid across the floor, and smacked into my legs.

I knelt down and let him lick my face. "Hey, my little babushka," I said. "Did you miss me?" Judging by the number of licks, I knew he had. I petted his wiry gray hair, and his little tail wagged with glee.

With Philippe at my heels, I did a quick walkthrough of the rest of the downstairs, making sure we were prepared for tonight. Rory and I were hosting yet *another* fundraiser. At least I think it was a fundraiser. We'd hosted so many events that year that they all ran together. If we weren't hosting, we were attending something. I had no idea how social one could be until I married Rory. Even as a practicing lawyer in our early years, he'd loved to go out on the town and say hi to people. Now that he was the mayor, we never stopped. He could shake a thousand hands a day, and it wouldn't be enough to satisfy his inner extrovert. For this reason, winning the mayoral election came so easily to him. His most amazing skill was that he didn't forget names. For every hand he shook, he knew the names of that person's family members. He could even remember the names of their pets.

Rory's unending craving for the support of other people was what started us on our downhill slope. His pursuit of a political career became his mistress, and I faded into the background. My not remembering which fundraiser we were hosting doesn't mean I was against helping people. Not at all! I was going through a lot, working my plan with everything I had in me, and trying not to acknowledge the deep pain in my heart. I had become a zombie. Fundraisers were a great thing, and as Rory and I hit the political world, I embraced helping on a larger scale. At first, I even thought Rory's new shoes as mayor were the perfect fit, and I was even more attracted to him. But hosting and attending those numerous events were certainly starting to wear me down.

I walked into the kitchen, where my team of University of Vermont culinary students were finishing up the hors d'oeuvres. My parents had instilled in me a love for the cooking process, and when I left the stage, I satisfied my desperate need for creativity by spending more time in the kitchen, creating another form of art. Fortunately, Rory and I were in a financial position that afforded me the luxury of not working outside the home unless I chose to do that. And in my case, I had chosen that time to live the life of a homemaker, putting healthy meals on the table and giving Jasper and Rory my full attention, giving them a rich and full life.

Sure, I could have had the city pay for caterers. In fact, that's exactly what Rory wanted me to do, but I found great pleasure in preparing the food for those events. Especially with our marriage becoming somewhat blurry, I fell even deeper into the culinary arts. Rather than hiring a caterer, I'd put together a team from the University of Vermont who shared my passion. Unlike many others, I, as the kitchen leader, didn't scramble at the last minute. I ran my kitchen like an admiral runs her ship. We still had the rest of the afternoon for detail work, but we'd prepped most everything.

I clapped my hands, and we did our pre-party lineup. Eager heads nodded as I ran through the checklist. We'd stuffed the

Castelvetrano olives with roasted garlic and Parmesan bread-crumbs, and the olives were ready to be deep fried at the last moment. We'd par-baked the baguettes. The onion tarts and the leek and mushroom croquettes were ready to bake in one of my three ovens. Bowls of spiced pecans, Ribiola-stuffed figs, and dips such as my to-die-for beet hummus waited in the fridge. In addition to a nice selection of wine, we'd made several pitchers of my eggnog, using my famous recipe. Despite all the work we'd put into making this long list of deliciousness, the kitchen was sparkling clean. I was an admiral proudly looking over my shipshape galley.

As I was about to thank my team and ascend the stairs to dress for the occasion, Rory appeared. Everyone turned. Though he was simply my husband, a regular guy, he was also the mayor, and people treated him to some extent as a celebrity. All eyes turned toward him as he approached me.

I feel the wind leaving my sails even as I introduce him to you for the first time.

Rory was still as good-looking as he had been when I'd married him. In fact, he was aging well. His gray sideburns and mild wrinkles gave him an attractive rugged look. That's why the fact that we hadn't slept together in more than a year grated on me. I still wanted him. Did he still want me? *That* was yet to be determined. He hadn't yet dressed for the evening and was still in loafers, jeans, and a polo shirt.

"Smells good in here," he said, bouncing his eyes from person to person and flashing his politician's smile. Stopping when he found my eyes, he asked, "Did you overdo it again?"

Rory didn't appreciate my efforts in the kitchen like many others did. He didn't *hate* my food. He loved eating it. But the closer he came to "game time," as he called it, the less he cared about food and such things, and the more he cared about us nailing our speech and creating an unforgettable party. One thing I hadn't considered when he first told me he wanted to run for mayor was that his appointment would mean I would also find a new role. Like the First Lady, a mayor's wife has tremendous responsibilities too. In his opinion, working in the kitchen had nothing to do with being the mayor's wife.

I didn't like the feel of his question, but I had no interest in a public joust, so I simply said, "I think your constituents deserve the best, and that's what we're giving them."

He nodded, knowing I'd won that one. Rory obsessed over many things, and if he became fixated on an idea—like that he needed me upstairs—he had a hard time letting go. He rubbed his hands together and almost walked away. I wished he had. Instead, his OCD won, and he said in a degrading and demanding tone, "I need you upstairs. We have a big night ahead." He glared at me and made a motion with his thumb, a command to follow him.

The admiral doesn't take commands well. As part of my plan to get him back, I'd been letting him get away with such comments. But not now, not in front of my staff. Not in front of the people who looked up to me. Going against my plan, I looked him right in the eyes and calmly said, "You do what you do best. I'll do what I do best. You may not appreciate our food, but I assure you the guests tonight will." Continuing with my own glare, I made a similar motion with my thumb and added, "Why don't you go upstairs and prepare yourself? Go put on your mayor cape."

Rory gritted his teeth. "Margot, stop playing house and get your ass upstairs. Right now."

How dare he? I was furious. Livid! I crossed my arms and stared at him with angry eyes. Through gritted teeth, I said with fire, "You're embarrassing yourself."

He bit his tongue, and I knew he was not interested in continuing such an embarrassing public display. At the same time, I wasn't sure he worried about what my "lowly" staff thought of him. Verifying my suspicion, he said, "The rest of these people can cut up your carrots and your celery and pour some ranch into a bowl. You have an *important* job to do."

I stepped toward him and put my finger to his forehead. "You can go fuck off."

You see, I was unraveling.

Rory's eyes bulged, and it was obvious by the red flushing of his cheeks that he was not only suffering from shock, but he was also embarrassed. No one speaks to the mayor that way. Oh, yeah? Well, no one speaks to Margot that way. This was how my plan began to backfire. Though I'd bitten my tongue for almost a year, I was losing discipline. Six months ago, I might have playfully saluted—and only to bring an end to it—have said, "Yes, sir," when he told me, as if I were an obstinate child, to get my ass upstairs.

Realizing how far I'd strayed from my plan, I took a deep cleansing breath and relaxed. I put my hand on his cheek. The girls in the kitchen didn't dare move, unable to avert their eyes. I knew I might enjoy a round of applause from my team if I punched that pompous ass right in his pompous mouth. Controlling myself, I patted his cheek and said, "Don't be nervous. I'll be up in just a minute, and we'll collect ourselves."

Rory nodded and left the room, and I heard him pounding up the stairs. Trying desperately to hide my plethora of emotions, I turned back to the ladies, and we finished our lineup.

Then I went to release some pressure.

"No one speaks to me that way," I muttered to Philippe as we left the kitchen. Being patient with Rory was growing increasingly difficult. What could I possibly do to calm down? I wasn't ready to face him again, so I stayed downstairs. I paced around searching like a crazy person for a way to find a release.

While glancing toward the bar in the corner of the living room, I found my answer. There was a beautiful garland with glass ornaments running along the face of the wooden bar, but I wasn't interested in my decorations at the moment. My eyes went to the lines of liquor bottles on the shelves behind the bar. I focused on a bottle of Scotch. Oh, I knew how to get him. The most apropos song in the world came to me like an early holiday gift. The words rose from my lips. "A spoonful of sugar makes the medicine go down, the medicine go down, the medicine go down."

I rounded the bar and poured two fingers of Scotch over a few rocks in a lowball glass. Humming my song, I walked into our laundry room and opened our utility closet, where we kept our medicine. I reached past the more commonly taken over-the-counter drugs like Advil and Pepto-Bismol and found the prescription antibiotic I'd taken to fight through a debilitating bout of strep throat a few months before. This pill's active ingredient was penicillin, a drug Rory was allergic to. Not so allergic, in a small dose, that he would die. I wasn't there yet. *Not yet!* But he would most likely break into hives and a terrible rash.

Philippe was sitting on his hind legs looking at me with wide-eyed wonder.

"Don't look," I begged. "This isn't my proudest moment."

He turned his head, as if working hard to translate my words.

I carefully pulled the gelcap apart. I shook one half into the glass of Scotch. "That should do it," I said. I stirred the contents while starting up my song again. "A spoonful of sugar makes the medicine go down."

It occurred to me as I left the laundry room that the Scotch might not be enough to conceal his poison. I looked at the brown liquid and then shrugged my shoulders. What the heck. I took a tiny sip. I never drink Scotch, but I knew that bitter taste wasn't normal. What could I do?

Only one answer. I rushed back to the bar and scanned our mixers. I removed from the shelf one of our mixology books written by a bartender in Manhattan and searched for Scotch. You wouldn't believe what I found! He had a drink called The Penicillin. The recipe called for lemon juice and honey-ginger syrup, which I didn't have and didn't have time to make, so I improvised. I have a thing for Domaine de Canton ginger liqueur and always have a bottle sitting around. I put in a splash and then dashed my melting cocktail into the kitchen. I said hello to my team, found a lemon, and squeezed a skosh into the drink.

As I gave my concoction one more stir, I heard Rory coming down the stairs. Those creaky steps had become warning bells. I met him on the last step and held out the drink.

"I've come to make a peace offering," I said.

Rory looked at the drink and said, "What's that?"

I didn't dare tell him the name of the cocktail. He was terrified of penicillin, having accidentally taken it a year ago to bad effect. Even the word would have turned him off. I said, "Oh, just a little Canton and Scotch. A twist of lemon. I thought it might make you feel better."

He thanked me and took the glass. I hoped he might apologize for earlier, but he didn't bring it up. No matter. As he enjoyed his first sip and gave a nod of approval, I felt much better. Mary Poppins better! Where, oh where, were my white gloves and umbrella?

"I'm sorry I snapped at you earlier," I said.

Rory savored another sip and replied, "Me too."

I kissed his lips, tasting the lemon and ginger. I told him I loved him, excused myself, and made my way up the stairs.

If he wanted to play his games, I was prepared to be his fiercest competitor.

2

THE DREAM KILLER

I am more than confident that no therapist, including my own, would recommend the pressure-cooker solution I'd embraced, but I'll be darned if it didn't work. As I climbed the steps to get ready, Philippe close behind, I wasn't nearly as angry. Maybe a hair annoyed, but I wasn't engrossed in fury. Rory often made rude comments, but I couldn't get hung up on those. Especially not if I were trying to pull him back to me.

Rory had a difficult job. I had previously thought his job as an attorney had taken all he had, but that job didn't even compare to his job as a mayor. The day he'd committed to running for mayor, he began running on overtime. Night and day. Day and night. Even in his sleep, he talked business and politics. This past year had been the steepest slope of his career. I had to support him, which meant that I'd needed to cut him some slack.

Until death do us part. In sickness and in health. When I'd married him, I'd promised to be his best friend and his partner and his cheerleader. I refused to let those promises slip away without a good fight. If being a great mayor and climbing to a US Senate seat would give him an outlet to fulfill his true potential, I wanted to be the partner who helped him achieve his goals. I knew he'd pay me back down the road. If I had to ignore a few verbal jabs and lonely nights, months, and even years, so be it. That's part of what love is about. That's a part of what marriage is about. When one of us is down, we're supposed to take turns lifting the other up.

But I was getting fed up. While I bettered myself, he worsened.

Our bedroom boasted fine antique furniture, including a stunning king-size bed made in Paris at the turn of the twentieth century. Philippe jumped onto the white duvet. Rory didn't want a dog in the bed, but you guessed it, I did. Before closing the blinds, I stared out a window overlooking the front yard. My eyes went right of the driveway, close to the tree line. That area is where I wanted to put a chicken coop, stage two of my plan to build what I liked to call Margot's Ark. Now that I'd persuaded Rory to let me adopt Philippe, it was time for the chickens. I dreamed about beautiful hens running around our property. I imagined going out to sing to them while collecting their eggs. For your information, I'm a vegetarian, not a vegan, so I do eat eggs and dairy. Anyway, I could almost see the birds out there, pecking in the snow. I could almost hear the rooster crowing. He wouldn't be a mean rooster. He'd be a sweet little rooster that would wake us in the morning with promises of a lovely day ahead.

My chicken-owner dream carried me away. I saw my ark coming alive out there in the snowy clearing. Sheep, goats, donkeys, and llamas. Many more dogs. Horses. If I could legally do it, I'd have zebras, lions, tigers, and bears. I didn't mind that our grass would be uneven and that we'd have to build fences. I wanted my ark. Knowing Rory, though, I'd only get so far.

I undressed and looked at myself in the tall mirror inside my walk-in closet. I still hadn't gotten used to the woman looking back at me. For all my life, I'd been curvy and plump. Not grotesquely overweight but enough overweight that I wasn't excited about wearing a swimsuit during summer vacation. This year, however, I'd dropped below my college weight. I was skinny with a flat stomach, and what I had considered to have been overly large breasts had settled into a gorgeous D-cup. I had it all. I couldn't figure out why Rory still hadn't noticed the new me. Not enough to come after me, at least. Lord knows, almost all the other males in town turned their heads when they saw me. I kept telling myself to be patient. You don't fix a marriage in a few months. But half of me was always on the verge of screaming, "I did all this for what? Nothing is getting better!"

I hadn't come to look like this without sacrifices, as in gargantuan sacrifices. It had been so long since I'd had a refined or starchy carbohydrate that my ribs showed. I needed to be careful that I didn't get too skinny! I missed all the good food in a big way. As often as we ate out, I missed ordering whatever I wanted, a practice I'd followed most of my life until this year of what felt like my year of starvation. Honestly, though, I will admit that the feeling of being slender warmed me up inside. It gave me a little kick in my step when I strolled down the street. I enjoyed being what some guys called a MILF. If you don't know what that is, please don't bother researching the term.

Along with this new killer bod, I'd chopped off my hair. Occasionally, over our years together, Rory had overtly hinted for me to go short. I suspected it had to do with his career. Everything he did had to do with how it affected his career. I secretly postulated that he had run a poll with the women at his office, and they'd suggested that, as the mayor's wife, I might look more dignified with short hair. Polls, polls, polls. He didn't make one decision without a poll. I wouldn't have put it past him to direct his people to run an actual poll using his constituents. Even if I asked what he wanted for dinner, he'd consider running a poll. He did notice the day I cut my hair, though, and his compliments made me happy. He didn't tear my clothes off, but at least he'd noticed.

To be truthful, he hadn't torn my clothes off in more than a year. The last time almost didn't count. It was around Thanksgiving, and our short stint of making love felt more like work. Though he never admitted to as much, his chore was dealing with getting undressed, hanging his clothes so they wouldn't wrinkle, and working his way to getting hard. For me, the chore was trying to believe he wanted me.

Put on your seatbelt, because I'm about to overshare. That's what I do, so you'd better get used to it. The fearlessly unfiltered, oversharing Margot is about to make you blush. Our first time making love, when he returned to New York, was mesmerizing. He could do things I only had read about in books. None of my boyfriends to that point had ever given me such monumental orgasms. As the years ticked by, we went from three times a week to once a week to once a month. Then I wasn't having orgasms. He would often go limp after a few minutes. I toiled for many years before I started using a vibrator, but once I was introduced to my favorite purple one, that well-endowed silicone member endured plenty of use, and I was sure to keep a ready supply of batteries.

I am not one of those women who doesn't need orgasms. I need orgasms like rabbits need other rabbits. I need orgasms like boats need water. If Rory would not give me what I needed, it was up to me to find an alternate method, and I wasn't inter-ested in being unfaithful and stepping outside my marriage to find a lover. I had no desire to have a sexual experience with anyone other than my husband. But I did want a safe, guilt-free outlet that needed no confession or request for forgiveness. Although it wasn't an ideal solution, a vibrator gave me the sexual release I needed.

I tell you all this to make my point that Rory wasn't caving easily, even with all the changes I had made. He was not coming back to me like I thought he would. Sure, I knew it would take time, but with a body like mine, why was he not jumping all over me? I knew women who were overweight but continued to be desired by their husbands and were sexually satisfied, so I realistically knew my new body wasn't the only reason why Rory should desire me, but I thought it should have helped to pique his interest.

When you're a mom, you let things slide. Men hadn't hit on me for years, but when I dropped the weight, my confidence rose, and men began hitting on me again. If I had taken off my ring, and if more than half the people in the city hadn't known who I was, I could've found a new man every day. That wasn't my goal. My marriage was important to me. I wouldn't betray my husband or make a mess of things and run the risk of losing my son's respect if an affair were to come to light.

In the bathroom, which I'd redone to create a much more elegant feel, I turned the brass knobs on my clawfoot tub, and hot water spilled onto the porcelain. I don't know when the following naughty habit started, but it's a habit in which I still happily indulge. Maybe it's not healthy, but life needs to be enjoyed. I reached for a half-full bottle of merlot from the shelf and poured myself a glass.

I slowly eased into the water, sipped my merlot, and closed

my eyes. I fell into another daydream. It was during my fantasies that I could find true peace. Before I ever dreamed of owning a chicken coop, I'd dreamed of owning and operating a bed-and-breakfast. Rory had shot down the idea before I could even get the full proposal out of my mouth. That's when I began to call him the dream killer, a name my close friends and I became fond of calling him.

Like convincing him about Philippe, I had learned that catching Rory at exactly the right moment was the key, like maybe when he was psyched after an important speech or after a journalist had written something wonderful about him in the newspaper. Sneaking in the idea of getting chickens might work this way, but the bed-and-breakfast was a different story.

Burlington, Vermont, could be one of the best places on earth to have a bed-and-breakfast, and I possessed the time and skills. I could have pulled it off. But if getting chickens was a hard sell to Rory, buying and running a bed-and-breakfast was an absolute "There's no freaking way in hell, Margot. Don't bring it up again." In fact, I think that's exactly what he said. All part of his OCD nature, which makes changing his mind almost impossible.

Still, when I closed my eyes, I often visited my cute little inn. I wanted nothing huge. I wasn't worried about what we could afford, and, at the same time, I wasn't worried about making tons of money. I wanted the pleasure of making people happy. I wanted a manageable place where I could pamper people with my china, silverware, attention to detail, and, most of all, my cooking. It would have been the perfect project to prepare for the coming empty nest that was not too far off in our future, even if I were the only one thinking about that future. Maybe that's why I pushed so hard to save my marriage. Jasper would be leaving home and heading off to college before long, and that day would pull back the curtain on the gaping black hole growing between Rory and me, ready to suck us up into infinite darkness. Who wants that?

Buying an inn could give us something fun to do. Rory had worked construction in college, so he could use some of his experience to help me put the place together. If he continued to become lost in politics—as he had been most of the time—I'd have something to do. I could immerse myself in the tiny details of keeping an inn and providing delicious meals. Maybe someday I could expand beyond offering breakfasts and do lunches and dinners once or twice a week.

Cooking for these get-togethers like the one tonight was fine, but I wanted a place where people would come for the food first, not for the crap spewing out of my husband's mouth. Feeding the walking dead who were chasing the next rung on the ladder was getting old.

The quiet in the house shattered as the dream killer's feet smacked the creaky steps. I opened my eyes and sipped my wine. A much bigger sip. Gulp, gulp, gulp.

I heard him tell Philippe to get off the bed. I was grateful that he hadn't snapped at my sweet little dog. Rory wasn't typically a hothead. His remark had been a quick, "Phil, you know better than that." Then Rory walked shirtless into the bathroom and approached the sink. Slightly disappointed, I didn't notice any hives or rashes. Maybe I should have used the whole pill. He didn't bother looking in my direction.

I wanted to say, "Hello, I'm the naked woman in here." Instead, I smiled and asked, "How are you feeling, honey? Are you ready?"

"You know it." I'm sure he revisited his checklist as he lathered shaving cream onto his face. The man shaved twice a day and always glistened. He could be the face of Gillette.

I sat up higher in the tub, revealing more of my body. Turning up the sexiness in my voice, I said, "You'll kill it, mister. Like you always do." Rory nodded, and I asked, "Is there anything I can do for you?" He shook his head. He wasn't remotely enticed by my subtle offer to give him an orgasm, and I translated his reaction to mean that he wasn't interested in giving me one either. A wave of defeat ran over me. Why couldn't he even turn around? What man doesn't want to see a naked woman?

I fought for patience and scrambled for my next move. Should I invite him into the tub? We had plenty of time, and we'd succeeded underwater before. As awkward as those times were, the memories still brought a smile to my face. I used to love it when he slipped into the bubbles and disturbed me from my dreams.

Now, though, he didn't care that his beautiful, now skinny, short-haired wife was sitting naked in the tub wanting him. He didn't care that I wasn't repulsive. He didn't care about my beautiful breasts and swollen nipples poking just above the waterline. I wanted to tell him to forget the damned razor, turn around, and drop his pants. *Show me what you got!* I didn't care if I received anything out of it. I'd be so thrilled just to give. Sure, I'd love an orgasm, but I would have happily given him a hand job, so he might remember what I can do for him. Any step toward an intimate physical relationship would be fine.

I knew, though, from experience, that there was no way we would have such an encounter. The Rory that I had married wasn't home. The politician Rory was in residence. Yes. The dream killer Rory was most likely here. The man I'd married? Not in this home. I sighed and closed my eyes again, returning to the daydream of my bed-and-breakfast, trying to let go of my frustrations.

I was imagining Philippe playfully running after a hen when Rory asked, "What are you thinking about?"

I almost told him the truth, but I knew where that conversation would go. Rory would turn his head and tell me to let it go. That there was no way we would buy an inn and take on a new project when his career was on fire. He had no time for such trivial business concepts when he was about to turn the state of Vermont over on its head. Like I said, his "no" was beyond firm on this one.

For most of the past year, I might have fed his ego with an ass-kissing answer. I might have told him I was thinking about what color tie he should wear or what dress I'd wear that might complement his look. I was, after all, his arm candy—his accoutrement. Everything I said and did needed to support his mission.

But the power of this pressure-release solution was softening. I was angry again, and it felt increasingly like my little passive-aggressive attacks weren't working like they used to. Okay, poisoning him might have been a length or two past a "little passive-aggressive attack." And even that hadn't worked! Almost like a medicine you take too often, my domestic remedies had lost their effect. No matter how much calm and peace my daydreams about the inn brought me, I couldn't shake the anger and utter frustration inside. Did I need to increase the dosage even more?

I felt confrontational, and even though I knew it wasn't the right time, I said rather truthfully, "I was thinking about chickens. I want chickens so badly. Can you imagine bringing a basket of fresh eggs into the kitchen every day? We'd have the most amazing breakfasts. Fried eggs with rich orange yolks. Frittatas that would bring tears to your eyes. French toast that would make your mouth water. Fresh pasta all the time.

Hmmm. We could raise Easter Egger hens, and the eggs would be a rainbow of colors. I'd do all the work. You wouldn't have to lift a finger. I could hire a contractor to build the coop." I felt like I was spitting out anything that came to mind. Being married to a politician meant that I had to work hard to get what I wanted. To that end, I realized I needed to appeal more specifically to him. I'd learned a few tricks while being married to Rory and knew I had to put myself in his shoes.

Verbally pivoting, I sat up and said, "Imagine when people visit. It's such a trend now to have your own chickens. It will make you, make *us*, seem more real. Real people. Weekend farmers. Not afraid to get our hands dirty. With this Whole Foods and farmers market movement, we'd be one of the early adopters to implement the program in our area. I could make deviled eggs and other things for our parties and brag about how the eggs had come from our own hens. I could name the hens after Broadway women, and your constituents will love us even more." I had to stop there and rest my case. I couldn't seem too desperate, or he might argue that I was being irrational.

Being a good listener and a good politician go hand in hand. For that entire diatribe, Rory hadn't said a word. In fact, he'd stopped shaving and turned around to listen. He was always good about letting the other person finish before he responded. If others weren't careful, they'd interpret his silence and slow nod as some sort of consensus, but that was rarely the case. He was preparing for his next debate, like the ones he'd been winning since his debate team debut in high school.

He wiped off some shaving cream that had dripped down his chest and finally granted me a response. In a placating tone, he warned, "Nice try, Margot. Please don't try to entice me by making owning chickens sound like a political issue. I see right through it. You can't bullshit a bullshitter. You know that." He sighed. "I'll tell you this right now. A few birds in our front yard will not put me in a senate seat. It would be just another distraction for both of us. We already have plenty going on. Honestly, we both know you will never stop. I let you adopt a dog and now it's chickens. After chickens, it will be a horse. Eventually, you'll want a damned elephant. I have no intention of allowing you to turn this place into a menagerie, and I'm putting an end to this whole idea of yours before it goes any further."

He sliced his hand through the air and continued, "I'm drawing the line, honey. I'm sorry. It seems like a fun little thing to you, but you're not thinking of the downside. Having chickens means feeding them and collecting eggs. Cleaning out the coop is easy enough in the summer, but what about when it's freezing cold and icy outside like it is now? What about when it's pouring down rain? You don't need me to tell you you're not a farm girl."

His last comment infuriated me more than anything he'd said in weeks. I could be a farm girl. He just wouldn't allow me to become one. In his mind, he didn't see me as an equal. He didn't see me as an independent woman. He was reducing me to child status. I wasn't afraid to get my hands dirty. I wasn't afraid of the cold.

I started to argue, but Rory wasn't finished and kept plowing ahead. "Worst of all, you can barely deal with a dying bug. You've been known to spend nearly an entire day trying to catch a spider in the house to set him free outside. How are you going to deal with a dead bird? These chickens...they die all the time. I can't have you going through a monthlong mourning period every time a hen kicks the bucket. I can already see you needing to have a funeral every time you lose one."

Wow, he wasn't coming around at all.

The dream killer strikes again.

My jaw tightened, and I pressed against the walls of the tub with my feet and hands. As my dream of chickens died in my heart, my blood simmered. I wanted to stand up and yell, "Why are you not having sex with me right now! How is that possible? I look better than I ever have, and you don't even notice me. You could have me every morning." I wanted to point to my body and say, "You could have *this* every morning! Look at me! Look at me!"

I remained quiet, though. I already knew how he would respond to such an outburst, and I didn't need to be further humiliated at that point. He'd tell me he didn't have time to make love and didn't have time to argue. Tonight was important. We could make love later.

Once he'd finished shaving and had patted his face with aftershave, he left the bathroom. We both knew silence was the best option at that moment. Sometimes it's best to walk away. Hearing his footfalls smacking the steps, I rose and climbed out of the tub. The pressure inside me was building, and I had to find a release.

Pulling on my robe, I entered the bedroom. Philippe rested on his doggie bed by the window. I patted my bed until he jumped up. That felt nice. One little victory.

The pressure was still building.

My eyes went to the television, and I realized what I could do to make the anger go away. I found the remote and turned on the television. I navigated to the recordings he'd made of his Buffalo Sabres games. Perhaps his only indulgence outside of work was his love for the Sabres. Rory would rewatch the matches several times and scream at the coaches and players as if he could have done it better. Rory had played hockey as a kid, which certainly didn't make him an expert, but he was absolutely obsessed with the Sabres and knew just about everything there was to know about them and their sport. He knew all their stats. Rory was a master of conversation, and I'd noticed that when he scrambled for something to say, the Sabres skated in to save the day. By the time he'd finished a rant, you'd almost have thought he could have single-handedly won the coveted Stanley Cup.

The Sabres were good that year, at least they had been for the first couple of months into the season. Rory had been busy though, so the games were stacking up in his digital library. He hadn't been able to analyze them like he'd wanted.

Guess what. He would never get that chance.

I deleted one game. The pressure eased out of me. I deleted another. A smile surfaced. Another. My shoulders dropped. By the time I'd deleted them all, I was suddenly in the holiday spirit and pranced to my closet whistling "Jingle Bells."

3

THE FUNDRAISER

Rory and I had hosted so many of these functions, from lunches, high teas, barbecues, cocktail parties, and dinners, that they began to run together. I felt like a windup doll. Wind me up, point me in a direction, and let me do my thing.

Tonight felt different, though. The wheels had come loose on my car, and I was becoming a liability. As far as my being a car, I wish I could say I was a Ferrari, but the station wagon that was Margot Simpson was about to screech across the highway on its axles, doing seventy. In my rearview mirror, I could already see the wheels breaking away from the car and rolling off onto the shoulder. What could I have done to tighten those lug bolts? Why wasn't my plan working like it should have?

The guests were due to arrive at six. My team and I had every last bit of food finished by five-thirty. Rory, on the other hand, never felt prepared. But once that first knock came at the door, he knew he had to be ready. On this particular evening, he ran around frantically looking for his phone. Did I mention that, earlier, I'd thrown it under the couch in his office? Naughty, naughty Margot! Every time I heard him spit a curse word into the air, I enjoyed a tiny flush of pleasure. I couldn't believe he didn't grab my phone and call his number so its ring would let him know where his phone was, but I suppose he was so frustrated that he didn't even think to do that. Even if he had, it wouldn't have helped. Naughty Margot had turned off the ringer! Eventually, he gave up looking, with a final string of curses that scared Philippe so much that our poor dog cowered and escaped upstairs.

Rory's team arrived a few minutes before the guests. My best friend and I often joked and called his team the harem. The dream killer's harem. Each of them came off as terribly nice, "terribly" being the operative word here. In this business of politics, even in the lower level of the mayor's world, everyone had an agenda. They might shake my hand and kiss my cheek and smile with apparent sincerity—even compliment my dress, my home, or my food—but I had to remember each of them had an agenda. I knew if I ever forgot that fact, they wouldn't hesitate to eat me alive.

Robert, the only man on Rory's team, arrived first. He and his wife stepped inside our foyer, and Robert dutifully commented on the brilliant Christmas decorations. His wife eagerly agreed with an aggressive nod. My husband and I dove into our first small talk of the night. Rory did what he does best and cracked the awkward silence with a slightly jarring joke about getting old. To my delight, I noticed red blotching on Rory's neck. Was my concoction working? Amidst the laughter following Rory's joke, the four of us broke apart, and I welcomed another of Rory's team.

If the harem had a leader, it was Kim. She didn't lead from a business role perspective, because she was too low on the totem pole. She ran social media and other technology-driven tasks that were best left to a younger generation. No, her crowning glory stemmed from her youth and annoying good looks. She had a face that made most men, including the married ones, stop and turn. I didn't think it was fair that women could look as good as she looked. She honestly didn't even look real, more like a character a programmer with dirty dreams had created for a video game. As I met her eyes, I did feel a twinge of pity for her. It surely couldn't be so great to look like her all the time. I couldn't imagine the stares and comments she'd unintentionally draw. Kim's husband fit her well. He was the male version of perfection. I felt zero attraction to him, though. I liked my men a little rough around the edges, nothing too perfect. I know what you might be thinking—why was I complaining about Rory if I wanted a man who was less than perfect? Well, he'd slipped a little too low on the spectrum, if you know what I mean.

Naturally, Kim was the one I always felt a little jealousy toward. It's not that I thought Rory would cheat. To repeat my earlier point, his only mistress was his political pursuit. I didn't consider him the cheating type, but he was a flirt, and that came with the territory of being a politician. He always knew what to say at the right time. If you plan to stay married to a politician, you'd better learn to cope with a certain amount of jealousy. As we all kissed cheeks, Kim giggled at Rory's silly comment about the weather, and it drove me crazy how he interacted with her. Nothing overstepping bounds, but when she spoke, he gave her his full attention.

Even though I looked as good as ever, Kim looked so much better than I did. I'd learned for certain that there was one thing I couldn't change. I could lose weight, and I could cut my hair, and I could be extra sweet, and I could nearly turn into a slave giving my spouse everything I have, but the one thing I could not do is reverse the aging process. On a side note, as you'll learn later, my best friend had tried to reverse the aging process, and I'm not sure it was working. Anyway, was I too old to be sexy anymore? Is your forties the decade when you stop having sex? That possibility saddened me.

The other three women in the dream killer's harem arrived before go-time. Rory's secretary Nadine was the last one in. She and I had always hit it off, and I liked her very much. One of the few genuine smiles I offered that night was when she entered with her husband. Nadine wasn't as striking as Kim, but she had these giant breasts that fought to jump off her chest. Every harem needs one, right? Or needs two? (Ha!) Thankfully, she wasn't one to flaunt her goods. Heck, I think even showing cleavage with those two monstrosities would have been too much of a statement for any political fundraiser. She always dressed conservatively, and that made me feel comfortable around her. If Rory ever did look at her boobs, how could I get upset? Shoot, I even looked at her boobs from time to time.

Jealousy wasn't as much of a factor for me when it came to Nadine, so she and I had become friends. It wasn't like we hung out all the time after she finished work or on the weekends. She was a little too young for that. But she and I typically found each other at cocktail parties and found comfort in our banter. She didn't enjoy political chatter either, so we were able to have real conversations. She shared my love for cooking, and she loved talking about the latest movies on the Hallmark Channel, which had been a very guilty pleasure of mine since I was a child.

As her husband fell into a hockey conversation with Rory, Nadine raised a green-and-red gift bag toward me. "We brought a little something for you."

"Thank you very much!" I said, accepting the gift. "You're the only one who brings me things."

"You're always hosting, it's the least I can do. Please open it."

I pulled the bow and reached inside. There's no mistaking the heavy glass of a wine bottle. Pulling it out by the neck, I examined the label and read out loud, "Fidélitas." I didn't recognize the producer, not that I was a wine snob by any means, but below the producer on the label it stated *Red Mountain Merlot*. I'd never heard of Red Mountain and had no idea where it was, but oh, my goodness, did I love merlot! And Nadine knew it. "You're so sweet," I said, and I meant it. "If you don't mind, this one is not getting opened tonight. I'll save it for a special occasion." I put my finger to my chin and asked, "Now where is Red Mountain?"

Nadine beamed. "Washington State. I didn't know about Red Mountain myself, but I stopped at that little place in town, near the Starbucks, and the owner said you might enjoy it."

"He knows my taste." Slipping the bottle back into the bag, I confessed, "I didn't even know they made wine in Washington."

"That's what I said! The owner said everybody in the know drinks Washington State wine, and he said this place, Red Mountain, is extra special. He said they grow some of the best merlot in the country."

I smiled. "Thank you. I look forward to trying it."

Those genuine moments during these get-togethers saved me sometimes. Every time I felt a little too bitter at having to politicize once again, I had an encounter that reminded me that not all people in the political arena were bad. Only a few bad apples—or grapes—often made it feel that way.

These fundraisers weren't like other social gatherings. You don't show up fashionably late. You arrive on time so you can take advantage of every minute shaking hands and making connections. Only a few minutes after seven, as the music of Mannheim Steamroller led us into the Christmas mood, our house filled with well-dressed men and women warming up from the cold, munching on my food, telling stories, laughing, and making their way into their desired circles. Lawyers and doctors were looking for new clients. Young enthusiastic men and women were looking for future votes. The seasoned were looking for further validation. Golfers were looking to find partners for their first spring rounds. Others were looking for new members for their respective book, bridge, or tennis clubs. These clusters of people filled our foyer, living, and dining rooms.

At just the right time, before everyone was too full or too drunk to pay attention, Rory gathered everyone into the living room. He found his spot in the open space between the crackling fire and where Jasper's shiny black Model D Concert Grand Steinway stood a safe distance away from the fireplace. As of late, I'd been covering the beautiful piano when we had guests, because two weeks earlier, I'd cringed when a drunk woman thought the top made a good coaster for her gin and tonic.

Rory and I had done so many of these fireside chats that he didn't even need to summon me. I assumed my place next to him and smiled. Forty or so people pushed their way into the living room, and as Rory patiently waited, the volume of their little conversations dwindled to near silence.

If he made love to me like he gave a speech, I'm not sure I'd ever leave my bed. Or that I ever could! He waited until all the guests had found their spots. His eyes bounced from one person to the next as he made each of them feel like it was his or her special night. He unleashed his rehearsed grin, and the remainder of noise in the room disappeared.

I used to love that handsome grin. It's part of what made me fall in love with him. I remembered seeing it for the first time while standing on that stage in New York. I remembered his kind wave. Oh, how I missed those days. Now, I had to swallow the bile that rose in my throat when I saw this repulsive gesture, because I knew it was the trademark of the politician who had impeded our marriage, the politician who had possessed the Rory I'd married.

Once the nervous energy had filled the silence, Rory reached out, took my hand, and "graced" me with that same smile. All for me! (Right? What a showman.) Remember, I had acted for half my life. I returned a smile that looked even more sincere than his own. No one could see the poisonous thoughts dancing like little devils behind my eyes.

As usual, Rory raised his free hand in the air, which wasn't necessary because everyone had already quieted, ready to listen. He'd once admitted that raising his hand before a speech gave the impression, or more accurately, the illusion, that he was swearing under oath, that any words that followed this powerful gesture came from his heart, and that any words that followed fell just shy of the Word of God.

God, or the politician, or the dream killer, everyone *but* the Rory I had fallen in love with, opened his mouth and showered the people with his wisdom. As he did so, I marveled at the hives forming around his neck. I could tell they bothered him, too, because every once in a while as he blabbered, he'd gone in for a scratch.

After a brief and apparently itchy monologue, Rory glanced at me, and I knew that was my cue. He said to the crowd, "Margot and I are so happy to welcome you into our home. You can probably guess who's responsible for all these beautiful decorations and this wonderful holiday food." What a hypocrite. Notice how he said, "holiday," not Christmas. He continued, "Margot is the Dick Cheney in this relationship. I'm merely a pawn in her game." He turned to me and added, "And I'm lucky as hell that she even lets me on the game board."

A round of obligatory laughter circled the living room.

Rory let the commotion die down before continuing. "Thank you, my love, for supporting me all these years. You mean more to me than you'll ever know." Did he know how to play his part or what?

I smiled a thanks and turned to the guests, our audience. It was my turn now. I said with a smile that could melt the Sabres' hockey rink, "Dick Cheney. Really? Who in the world still makes Dick Cheney references? That was so five years ago." The guests grinned. I had them right where I wanted them. "And please don't tell me I look like some old man." The guests exploded with laughter. I'd won that round. I felt oh, so comfortable speaking in public and enjoyed performing again. If Rory wanted to play, I could too. I said, "I'll avoid any George W. comparisons or hunting-accident jokes and just tell you that, though my husband drives me crazy sometimes, this man cares about you. All of you. He cares about this town. We're all lucky to have him." A Tony-award nomination was surely in my future.

Though I had graced a stage or two in my day, I was still learning from Rory. The first thing he always did when giving a speech was to thank someone else. That's why he'd put the attention on me. He was establishing that he was a selflessly generous man. Tonight wasn't all about him. In return—though I was sincere—I thanked my kitchen staff, who had lined up in the back. After the applause, Rory and I waxed on for a moment about the charity.

Like I mentioned earlier, I can't for the life of me remember the details. I don't want you to think of me as a selfish disingenuous hag. Every charity did matter, but I was dealing with my own demons. My marriage was a catastrophe. My yearlong plan to get Rory back was going awry. I was holding on with everything I had, hoping and praying that Jasper hadn't noticed how bad his parents' marriage had gotten. For some silly reason, my Christmas wish was that Rory and I would have it all worked out by the time Jasper returned from his music camp in Texas. That hope was fading into impossibility.

Because this whole bit of banter had become our schtick, I knew what was coming, and I prepared mentally. Rory said to his congregation, "Would you mind if I ask something of my wife? You might know that I found this lovely being on a Broadway stage. Almost unfairly, I stole her from a very promising career." He turned to me and asked, "Margot, would you mind singing a little something for us before we return to our conversations about the amount on the check we'll write tonight?"

I remember wishing that Rory wanted to hear me sing. Like he used to. I wished his request hadn't become part of our schtick.

Everyone clapped and cheered encouragement as I thought about what I might sing. I hadn't prepared but didn't need to. I was never short on songs. When the clapping stopped, I rested my hand on the piano. As I'd grown accustomed to doing, I stared at a spot on the black cover and breathed in a few breaths. Once I felt the character awaken inside me, I raised my head to the crowd and sang a jazzy, up-tempo version of "Santa Claus Is Coming to Town." Halfway through, I began snapping my fingers and, by the end, the guests were all singing along with me.

Rory and I had them in the palms of our hands.

As usual, shortly after our speech, Nadine and I found

each other and drank wine in the corner. She made a comment about how great the food was, and I told her I hadn't been able to try it because of my diet. She encouraged me to keep doing what I was doing because it was working so well. She was even nice enough to ask the details of the diet, as if she needed to lose a pound. My diet was no secret, and I happily shared. "Just don't eat starchy or refined carbs. No bread, rice, potatoes, flour. Nothing enjoyable. Actually, just don't eat. If you're hungry, eat air. There are no calories in air." I feigned taking a bite out of the air in front of us and chewed.

Nadine laughed until tears ran down her cheeks. After we'd exhausted diet talk, I asked, "What do you think you'll do after this job?"

She shook her head. "I try not to look too far into the future."

"That's a good point. You're so much younger than I am, but when I was around your age, I felt like I had everything figured out, and then I met Rory, and the whole thing blew up in smoke. Not in a bad way. It's just that when you're in your..." I almost guessed an age but held back. "When you're so young, you think you have it all figured out. The world all makes sense. Then one little event can change everything. Just like that. So, take it from me, you're right in answering the way you did. Don't look too far into the future." I raised a finger. "But we all know working in politics requires a certain amount of foresight. What if Rory doesn't win the next election? What if he ends up running for senate?"

Nadine shook her head, as if she'd spent plenty of time pondering the thought. "I hope he'd take me with him. He's a great boss, and I think he's a great politician. He's been good for our city."

"Answered like a politician. Maybe you need to be the next mayor."

She and I laughed, and we both knew she could say nothing more than the best about my husband. I might have thought her kind comments about him were too flattering, almost like she was attracted to him, but *everyone* in his office bathed him with compliments. For that matter, everyone in Burlington did!

From his coworkers' comments and what I'd seen, Rory was a good boss. He fought to get his staff raises and more vacation time. He didn't ask more of them than he did of himself. He always had a smile on his face. Never raised his voice.

A little later, after hiding in the kitchen with the team for a while, I wandered through the living room looking for a new circle to join. While most of the guests enjoyed the good food, I chewed on another bite of air.

I spotted Rory talking to Kim, you know, the harem leader. The one with the video-game face. I didn't know where Kim's husband was, but Rory made her laugh again. I hate to seem like the jealous type. I really do. I know he was being a good boss, just being friendly, and there's nothing wrong with making people laugh. However, inside my heart, I longed for my husband to make *me* laugh again. I wanted him to *want* to make me laugh. Rory said something apparently even funnier, and that's when Kim smacked him on the shoulder and nearly collapsed in a fit of laughter.

A pain surfaced in my chest.

4

MISMATCHED SHOES

Once the guests had left, and the house had been cleaned, I retired to my room—my sanctuary. As if Philippe liked these entertaining obligations even less than I did, he was already up there, passed out on his back in his bed. Rory had invited a couple of key figures to stay for one more drink and was entertaining them in his office.

The pressure inside me became unbearable, pushing up against my ribcage and unsettling my stomach. I beelined it to Rory's closet. His OCD nature came alive in his closet. The collar of each hanging shirt had to face left. He'd trained me well in this regard, since I was the one who hung most of his clothes. In addition, he required color coordination, a wave of hues graduating from whites to light blues and into the darker blues. Pinks to reds, grays to blacks.

Until this week, most of what I'd been doing had gone undetected. That was the point, right? I wasn't looking to declare war on him. In fact, I was going for the exact opposite. If I was looking for any sort of reaction at all, I just wanted him to think he was losing his mind a little. A misplaced item, a deleted DVR game, a missing towel, a random allergic reaction. Little things that would drive him crazy but wouldn't point a finger at me. More and more though, I was slipping into a dangerous game in which he'd know I'd been the culprit, a discovery that would defeat the entire purpose of my mission to become Superwife.

Still, if he figured out I was guilty, I hoped he would only see my subtle sabotage as mere errors in my programming, not intentional jabs against him.

Revisiting what I had seen downstairs, I cringed that video-game Kim had found him so funny and had smacked him on the shoulder. I tried to tell myself Rory was just being Rory, but that helped a total of zero percent. I picked up an overly starched, light blue shirt, twisted the hanger around so that the collar faced left, and hung the shirt between two white ones. Ah, a little tiny breath of satisfaction. I removed a white shirt with red stripes, rotated the hanger, and placed it between two dark blue shirts. I could almost hear the pressure release on that one. I performed this inconceivable act three more times. Any more and I thought he'd figure me out. I was just looking for that subtle scratch of the head, dip of the chin, or low grunt that signified things weren't right in his world. I hoped he wouldn't even bring it up. Even he knew we must pick our battles in marriage.

I looked down at the closet floor. Rows of shiny business shoes lined the racks, each pair angled with care. On the floor were his more casual tennis shoes, slippers, and clogs. Even those were lined up almost too neatly. With great courage and daring, I reached down and switched a left slipper with a right black polished shoe. I let out a chuckle. This little game was satisfying. Dare I do another? Why not! This move had to be less drastic though. I switched a left brown loafer with a lighter brown loafer. Subtle, but still effective as far as satisfaction delivery. If he'd caught me at that moment, he would have lost his mind. The pure joy on my face would have hurt his feelings. In one last untoward act against his shoes, I picked up his tennis shoes and tied three knots in a row with one lace. I pulled them tight, so he'd have to use tweezers to untie the knot.

It still wasn't enough. Why not keep going until I had returned to normal? After the food I'd fed his constituents and the lovely Tony Award performance I'd delivered, he owed me at least that amount of joy. His allergic reaction wasn't severe enough to knock down all the dominoes.

I looked around the room, searching for another move. As was his preference, the bed was perfectly made. Actually, I must admit I also like a well-made bed. While he appreciated the discipline of the act, I enjoyed the art of making the bed. If you've ever pulled back the cover and top sheet of a bed at the Ritz-Carlton, you know what I mean. *If* I ever ran my very own bed-and-breakfast, people around the country would talk about their sleep experiences.

Being a vegetarian, I didn't use goose down, but I'd found a company that made nearly perfect alternatives. Four pillows rested against the long custom-sized bolster that ran along the antique king-size headboard. As is customary, the openings on the pillow cases pointed away from the center. A year ago, I'd unintentionally messed up the direction and accidentally faced them inward. Rory had about lost it. While whistling a Christmas song, I rotated his two pillows.

With a modicum of pressure still lingering, I searched the room until a perfect solution came. How had I never done this one before? I went to his tidy bedside table, picked up the digital clock, and added fifteen minutes to the time. Not enough of a time change that he'd immediately notice, but he would eventually discover the discrepancy, and it would grate on his nerves. Oh, how I liked grating his nerves! His nerves were like a chunk of Parmigiana Reggiano in my right hand, and every time I ran that block of cheese along my grater, I felt more at peace.

Finally, feeling almost back to normal—if anything about me that week was normal—I slipped into a nightgown and climbed into our comfy bed. Philippe approached the side and looked up at me with the most adorable face. Without a second thought, I patted the bed and gave him permission to board. My lovely dog found great pleasure not only in being on the bed, but also in crawling under the covers. As you can imagine, Rory didn't care for this move at all. With a shrug of my shoulders and a curling of my mouth, I lifted the white duvet and sheet, and Philippe—my grand prince—snuck inside and settled along my leg.

When I heard the burglar alarm being armed and then Rory climbing the stairs, I braced myself for his reactions. I may have gone a little overboard tonight with releases, and I hoped he might be too drunk to notice. Sadly, though, like the best of politicians, he was always just a little more sober than everyone else. I imagined he'd poured himself a glass of Scotch at least a finger or two shorter than those of the other two men who'd hung around to hear him proselytize.

Rory entered the bedroom with a bright smile on his face, but he wasn't drunk. His smile came from the high of all the attention his guests had bestowed upon him. Honestly, I think he'd rather give a good speech than receive a blow job. Hands down. I don't even think he'd have to think about it.

I feel like I'm once again making him sound like a prick.

And he could be one. That week especially. I wasn't the only one unraveling, though. While my unraveling had to do with losing control of my plan, his unraveling had to do with losing himself in his hyper-focus and forgetting his priorities. Trust me. If I caught him on the right day, when he wasn't as stressed, he'd happily and truthfully admit that his family held higher priority than anything else in his life, including his political aspirations.

I think his unraveling was nothing new in the political world. All around us, politicians are falling apart. They start out intending to help people. They're bright-eyed, enthusiastic, and full of ambition, and they know they have a talent for leading, so they choose the route of politics. They believe they can make a difference. They not only want to, but they believe they can help their neighbors, the rest of their city, their entire state, or maybe even the whole country.

Somewhere along the way, they lose their compass. Their life becomes full of tactics and not strategies. Focusing on the next vote becomes more important than focusing on what matters. They tell themselves that winning one more election will give them the ability to do so much more. They break the promises they made to themselves. Compromise their morals. They tell tiny little lies. They might expect a few favors. They might accept a few favors. Rory had never admitted to such, but I knew he wasn't as clean as he had been when we first married.

Who was I to judge, though? Most of us lose our way, even if only for a brief time. I, as his partner, needed to guide him and help him return to that bright-eyed and giving young man he used to be. That man from the past also loved the hell out of his wife and son. Bonuses all around.

"I found my phone," he announced, and that helped

explain the grin. I thought it might just have been frozen on him after forcing it for so long in front of his audience.

"Oh, good," I said cheerfully. As if I cared at all.

"It was under the couch." He shook his head. "I have no idea how it got there."

Oh, I do, I thought, but said, "You've been a mess today. It's hard to keep track of things."

"True. I had some kind of allergic reaction earlier too. Had to go take some Benadryl halfway through the night."

"What could that be from?" I asked innocently. "I hope you're feeling better."

Rory raised his hands, palm sides up to chest level. "I have no idea. I hate having to take that stuff, though. It knocks me out. It robs me of my personality" He changed the subject. "I thought tonight went well. *You*, my love, did great. I don't know where I'd be without you." I wished he meant those words, but by that point in our relationship, I was skeptical of any praise at all. I muttered a thanks and returned to my book. He walked to the end of the bed and put his hand on my foot. He shook it, making physical contact with me, but nothing really intimate. "You and I are dangerous together."

There it was. The truth. We weren't lovers anymore. At least not right now. We were colleagues. Roommates and colleagues. Coworkers. Teammates. The power couple of Burlington goes for the win! Ugh. What I wanted was some cuddle time. Even a hug would have been nice. Not a freaking shake of the foot! Not a high five. Not a towel swat on the butt in the locker room. I'm not your power forward, Rory. Do I look like I'm wearing ice skates?

Gosh! Was I the only woman in the world who wanted to be seen?

Rory undressed in front of his closet, methodically hanging

his belt, tie, and slacks. He didn't scratch his head or grunt as I'd hoped he would, but he pulled out and rearranged each one of his shirts and returned its hanger and color to its proper location.

If committing my little acts of attrition brought satisfaction, seeing him discover them and being forced to correct them was pure rapture.

Rory shook his head as he rearranged his shoes. How had he noticed so quickly? I could go weeks without noticing a mismatched pair of shoes in my somewhat-organized closet. Even if I were to notice an imbalance, I wouldn't bother fixing it for a while. I wondered so desperately what my husband was thinking. Did he think he might have Alzheimer's? Was he worried that age was finally taking its toll? Did he suspect me even in the slightest?

After he'd brushed his teeth, he returned to the bedroom and asked, "Do you mind if I watch the game for a little while?"

I was feeling better by that point and ready to continue being the awesome wife and partner I'd committed to being. I said, "Absolutely, sweetie. You deserve it."

I thought he might give me another foot shake for that one. Maybe a thumbs-up. Actually, if he'd given me a thumbs-up, I would have smacked him six ways to Sunday. As I was learning the hard way this week, I have my limits.

Rory didn't make much of a gesture at all. A simple head shake and a move to the remote, which meant he agreed. He deserved to watch the game for a while. Have I mentioned that I hate hockey?

As he stood there by his side of the bed and navigated to our recordings, I slipped deeper into the covers. I might have to pull them over my head to keep from being discovered. Philippe passed gas, though, which stopped my retreat. I put my eyes on the book. Rory still hadn't noticed that my little prince rested peacefully under the covers.

"What the hell?" he muttered.

Though, for all I knew, I might have been looking at my book upside down, I stared at it like it was my job. I tried so hard not to smile. He cursed, and I peered over the pages to acknowledge his frustration. "What's wrong?" I asked.

He turned to me. "I can't find my games. I swear they were here this morning."

"That's strange," I said, going back to my book.

In a rare act of losing his temper, Rory cast the remote to the floor and cursed again. Standing near his side of the bed, he asked, "Are you sure you didn't delete my games? They were here, damn it."

Even though I was guilty as charged, I didn't like being accused. This accusation unleashed an eruption of emotions, and I gritted my teeth and side-eyed him. He was probably waiting for me to admit guilt. It wasn't just the jealousy from the episode with Kim that I felt. Suddenly, all the fury and anger and fear that had been raging inside me came to life and shook every molecule of my body. I told myself to breathe through it. *You've made it this far, Margot. Don't collapse now!*

This self-awareness helped me grasp control mere seconds before I spat venom at him, even though his claims against me were justified. He stared at me, waiting for a confession. He was probably ready to unleash hell on me as punishment. I breathed and sought control. Oh, that venom though. My rage forced me to shake under those sheets.

I turned my head to him, ignored his question, and said, "You were an asshole to me in front of the kitchen staff today." I set my book down and dropped my head to the pillow. It felt good to tell him like it was, for once. How in the heck had I buried all these feelings for so long? Mismatching a pair or two of socks and shoes suddenly felt like an absurd way to find happiness.

Rory looked at me like I'd accused him of cheating. His eyes shot toward the ceiling and then back to me.

I could feel the anger boiling up between us. No doubt we'd both been biting our tongues lately. I saw the fire burning in his upper cheeks.

I don't give the man enough credit. Rory caught himself before he fell into my trap and into a game he knew he'd never win. His brow smoothed as he answered politely, "I know I let you down. The moment I said it, I wanted to apologize."

"You should have."

"I know, I know. It's hard to admit you're wrong when you're supposed to be right all the time. If it had been just us, I swear I would have said sorry. I knew I'd crossed a line."

"You should especially apologize in front of others. No one is ever going to disrespect you for loving and respecting your wife. And no one expects you to be right all the time." *Are you kidding me?* I thought.

In either a beautiful turn to honesty or one of his greatest performances of all time, he put both hands on the bed and said, "I've been a little distracted lately. I know that I can be a jerk sometimes. Please, please take nothing I say to heart. I was just nervous about tonight. If you'd like me to, I will be happy to say something to everyone."

"I'd like that. You should do it. I'd like for you to call every last one who worked in the kitchen today and apologize."

"Consider it done."

Gosh, that felt good. Powerful. Satisfying.

Was Rory telling the truth? I felt like I always asked myself this question. He always knew how to put on the charm when he needed to. Was it fake every time or was this the real thing? He stood there for what felt like forever looking at me. After a couple of minutes, he whispered a sorry.

I decided that he was telling the truth. That he was sincere. That he needed some forgiveness, and I needed to cut him a little slack. I said, "I'm sorry too."

He walked over to my side of the bed, and that's when he noticed Philippe's snout poking out from under the covers. Rory didn't lose his temper. He shook his head and asked, "Is this you crying for help? Is this you telling me I'm being a bad husband?"

God, he was good. I went from all the anger in the world to completely being at peace and in love with this man again. Almost like a pouty little girl, I nodded. For crying out loud, I had reduced myself to a child.

He asked, "Did you delete my games as part of this stance?"

Suspicious of his motive, I took a chance and nodded again.

He smiled and said, "You matter more than my games. I didn't mean to be a jerk today. Sometimes I take you for granted, but I don't mean to. He leaned down and kissed my cheek, and we hugged. This is why I didn't want to lose him. When I could wake him from his daydream, when I could pull the old Rory out of the politician, he was so warm to be with.

While he tried to glean more Sabres information from a sports channel, I dove back into my romance novel. Philippe climbed out, of his own accord, and found his bed on the floor.

I was smiling inside. So much so that after a little while, I started to think dirty thoughts. Not the thoughts you're thinking. Not thoughts of how I could secretly wage more wars on Rory. I had actual sexual feelings surfacing. It didn't hurt that, after a book's worth of cat and mouse, the woman in my novel was about to have sex with the man of her dreams. I couldn't turn the pages fast enough. Ah, the games we humans play.

I turned to my husband. Rory held his hands behind his head with his elbows flailed out. He was falling asleep. All our years flashed before me, and I smiled. I felt proud that I could see past the yucky parts of this man and still cling to what we had and could have again. I whispered that I loved him, and he said the same back.

I reached over and touched his hip under the sheets. It had been so long since I'd done something so bold that I almost felt uncomfortable. I feared rejection, but I held my ground. He opened his eyes and smiled. I dragged my fingers toward his midsection and found his member, or as I was guilty of calling it against his will, Li'l Rory. Sorry. T.M.I. should be my initials.

I hadn't touched Li'l Rory in quite a while, and as the not-so-little guy responded, I slid closer to my husband. In a humiliating barricade from love that I had feared, however, Rory pushed my hand away and said, "Not tonight. Please. Maybe tomorrow. I'm so tired. I just...I'm sorry."

I retracted my hand so quickly that it was almost as if Li'l Rory had become a poisonous snake about to strike. But I calmly replied, "Okay."

As a peace offering, Rory reached over and kissed my cheek. "Tomorrow, for sure. Please don't read anything into it. I'm just so—"

"I know," I said. "You don't have to apologize. I'm tired too."

But I was tired for different reasons. I was sick and tired of our life.

5

MY BEST FRIEND

Before Rory slipped out of bed the next morning, I thought he might at least snuggle with me for a moment. Some sort of loving encouragement after monumentally dissing me. I didn't even get a kiss. Li'l Rory might as well shrivel up and die. Rory didn't need that useless appendage anymore.

Still feeling awful, I sat up, rubbed my eyes, and glanced around the room. Rory had set out his work clothes on the chair next to our bed. I noticed his black socks curled up into a ball. My first act of the morning would be a grand victory. I unraveled the socks and walked over to his drawer. I found a pair of navy socks and unraveled them as well. Pairing one black and one navy sock together, I laid them on the chair. The shades of black and navy were so close together that he might not notice it all day, but I would know that I had the first win.

I thought of one more move to brighten this sexless day. While he showered, I snuck into the bathroom and removed the two towels from the rack. He hated to step out of the shower and find there wasn't a towel handy. Well, he would hate it today for sure. If he didn't want to share his penis, then he could dry off with the bathmat for all I cared!

Downstairs, I followed my routine. I put on a pot of water, placed a paper filter into the Chemex carafe, and pushed the grind button on our burr grinder. As the machine ground thirty-six grams of freshly roasted, single-origin beans, I went to the fridge to search for a bite of protein. I needed to eat more than air this morning. I needed to start my day with something of some substance. I found a boiled egg and ate half. A whole would have been too much. You couldn't look like I did eating a whole of anything.

"Good morning, dear," Rory said, coming into the kitchen as I sat down with my cup of coffee a few minutes later.

"Hi," I said, forcing some enthusiasm into my voice.

He poured himself a cup and topped it with organic cream. I wasn't even adding cream to my coffee anymore. Couldn't start the day with carbs or sugar. Black coffee for this skinny girl.

"I have a giant day today," he continued. "Tossed and turned all night thinking about how I would accomplish everything. I swear it never stops. What are you doing today?"

"Well," I said, thinking about it for the first time, "I'm meeting Erica in a little while."

Rory nodded, knowing he needed to tread carefully. He didn't like my best friend. In fact, he'd often said I was a different person after hanging out with her. He bit into a banana and said, "Don't let her rub off on you too much. I like you just the way you are." I almost lied and told him she was coming over for dinner tonight but decided that would be too cruel. Last time we'd tried that, we'd all barely gotten out alive.

He didn't say anything about the towels. I wondered if he was losing patience with me, wondering if I was off my game.

When I rose to top off my cup, I confirmed that he was wearing mismatched socks. Would he go all day like that or would one of his harem girls notice and save him? If she did, what the heck would she have been doing looking at his ankles! And if he knew, it would drive him crazy wondering how many people had noticed his embarrassing mistake. He'd probably send a harem girl out to buy new socks!

Nevertheless, the little victory was immensely satisfying. I smiled brightly and walked up to him as if he hadn't rejected me last night. A rejection, mind you, not too long after he'd tickled the fancy of the prettiest girl in the room, a woman he'd see again shortly at the office. I let all that go and gave the dream killer a peck on the cheek. I said, "Let me know if I can pick up the slack in any way."

"All right, all right, you don't have to placate me. I know you have your hands full too."

I put my hand on his shoulder. "Sweetie, this year is about you. I'll have my years, but right now, we're going for something big. For you. That's okay with me. When you win, I win."

He smiled and kissed me on the forehead. There's my Rory.

On his way out the door, I noticed the tiny fold I'd purposely ironed into the back of his collar. Those little things were no big deal, but when you're in public office, people do notice every detail. There he went, off to set the world on fire with mismatched socks and a misplaced crease in his collar. He had no idea. I hoped that one day we'd laugh at the things I'd done in an effort to save our marriage.

∽

"OH, I know you didn't have more work done," I said, bursting through the doors of our favorite Vietnamese nail salon, escaping the bitter cold.

My best friend Erica was already in one of the leather chairs, sipping on sparkling wine, while a technician wearing a surgical mask washed her feet in a basin. Another technician worked on a customer several chairs down.

I hung my jacket on the rack and walked toward Erica.

She looked at me like I'd insulted her, but I knew I could get away with it. That's why we were best friends. We were both bulls in a china shop, and we'd been born without filters. When we were together, there were no lines you couldn't cross. At least mostly. We'd gotten in our tiffs over time, but I never treaded carefully around her. Truth was, until Rory's public life, I never tiptoed on glass around anyone. But I'd learned, over the past few years, to remember that I represented the city of Burlington as the mayor's wife. As dull as it sometimes was, I at least tried to run my words through a quick check before letting them leave my tongue.

Not with Erica, though. She and I go way back. She and I gave birth to sons at about the same time. For a long time, Jasper and her son were great friends, but they drifted apart as Jasper moved more into the music crowd. There was nothing bad between them, but they didn't share a lot in common and didn't hang out like they used to when they were younger. Erica and I, however, were inseparable.

When you move to a new town, you say goodbye to everyone. I'd lived in New York quite a while and had left a lot of good friends. It was difficult saying goodbye, and it had been hard to establish myself in Burlington. I met people all the time, but it took a while to make connections. When I'd first moved to Burlington, Rory hadn't planned his political career yet, but his law practice was up and running, and he was socially active. I think he knew politics were in his future. So, yeah, I met tons of people and lots of women, and I participated in book clubs and bridge clubs and all that jazz, but it wasn't until I had Jasper that I met other moms. Being a mom defined me, so connecting with other moms gave me much more intimate and easy relationships.

Erica and I met at our sons' daycare. Since I'm not the shyest person in the world, I started the conversation. We talked about mom things—the best places to buy kids' clothing, the best doctor, what to do with the kids every day until school starts, our favorite books and toys.

Rory had gotten along with Erica's husband, and the four of us sometimes had done couples things together. Then, about the time the boys were turning eleven, Erica's marriage fell apart. Not a gentle falling apart like mine with Rory. Erica's marriage became extremely volatile. The couple could not agree on anything, and they slogged through a vitriolic divorce. I was there for Erica in every way. I had the attitude that to be a good friend, you needed to be there when the other one reached the worst of her valleys. Most of the time, all Erica needed was someone to listen to her. I'd stood by a sad woman for two years, and she loved me for that.

Last year, however, Erica had found a man on *Match.com*. I could hardly believe it. She'd spent months going out on disappointing dates, and she would tell me the most hilarious stories. We would enjoy a mani-pedi or have lunch at the club, and she would split my side with stories about the awful guys in Burlington I couldn't believe existed. I never thought she'd find anyone again. In fact, seeing her frustrations with the dating scene supported my case that I could never leave Rory. I didn't want to be alone forever.

Then, one day, Erica met the love of her life. Well, the second love of her life. Her son even liked him. I could go on, but this story isn't about Erica. You need to know about her, though. If you get to know me well enough, you'll hear plenty of great Erica stories. We had a long future together and looked forward to future experiences.

Together, we'd been visiting this same nail salon for years. It shares a parking lot with Target, Marshall's, and a few other great spots where we could enjoy a full day of therapy.

I stepped up into the chair next to Erica. "Don't even try to tell me you didn't get any work done. Oh, my God."

"I have no idea what you're talking about," Erica said, both of us knowing she was full of it. When I'd first met her, she had been so prim and proper, but after her divorce, she had done whatever she'd wanted to do. It was like her husband had kept her on a leash, and when she broke free, let me tell you, she broke free. She'd vacationed in Vegas by herself. She'd go on rock 'n' roll cruises. She'd spend tons of money on makeup, perfume, and any number of girlie things. And she'd gotten a few body parts tucked, pulled, and stretched, if you know what I mean. She hadn't gone overboard, but she was getting there. Between her alimony, child support, and her new profession of selling real estate, she apparently had plenty of spending money on hand.

Erica was my age, but with those little procedures she pointlessly denied, some subtle changes had been made to her appearance, and I suddenly realized I'd been wrong in my earlier assessment that the aging process can't be slowed down. Looking at Erica, it was evident that at least the appearance of slowing down the aging process can be achieved, but I thought it could still come back to bite her in the end—perhaps with a vengeance. I had no intentions of having plastic surgery.

Besides the fact that I'd recently read about people actually dying as the result of plastic surgery procedures having gone wrong, I feared, more than anything else, that I'd turn out to look like one of those celebrities who'd had one too many procedures and showed up on the covers of magazines on the racks in the grocery store checkout lanes. They looked younger, but they might as well have tattoos on their faces that read, "I had work done because I wasn't comfortable with who I truly am." Some of them almost looked like caricatures of their former selves, because the procedures had been so badly botched. So is it really necessary to blurt out or deny the "work?" Don't you love the word "work" in this instance? There's something so trendy about it. No, I don't get "work" done, but I don't judge anyone who does. You do you, as Jasper likes to say.

Erica was dying her hair. I'd seen those grays disappear a few years ago, giving way to a much darker brown. Sometimes she wore too much makeup, which was another thing I wasn't afraid to point out. She must have been more terrified than I was of getting old. I guess she'd already gotten a feel for divorce and had no intention of letting that happen again. Her "work" had been tasteful so far, and I so hoped for her sake that she didn't lose control.

"I haven't seen a forehead with fewer wrinkles since Jasper was four years old," I said.

Erica fluttered her brown eyes. "The dear Lord blessed me with fine skin."

I rolled my eyes. "And a very fine doctor."

She smiled devilishly. "Very *fine*, indeed. If my new husband ever leaves, I know who I'm going after next. The man has magical hands the size of tennis rackets." I knew she was joking, so I let her cheating reference slide.

One of the technicians welcomed me with a glass of sparkling wine. Do I sound like I drink too much? I feel like I'm oversharing my weaker habits. For the record, I used to go to the gym—occasionally. But why go to the gym? If I lost any more weight, Rory wouldn't "see" me because I'd disappear. Oh, I meditated—as in, I used to. I read self-help books—as in, I read them in college. You see, I was healthy—as in, healthier than some. I picked a light red nail color, and the technician went to work.

Turning to Erica, I said, "Dare I ask how your love life is going?" I already knew her answer would make me jealous, but not like Kim-in-Rory's-office jealous. It was okay to be a little jealous of your best friend. Erica smiled at me with explosive eyes. I waved my hand at her. "Maybe I don't want to hear about it."

"Oh, you do, my friend. You do. I can't believe I've gone all these years without satisfaction. Like Mick-Jagger satisfaction. Honey, he does things to me that, honest to God, make me shiver. If I keep screaming like I do, there's a good chance we'll be kicked out of our neighborhood."

I shook my head. Did I need to hear this right now? "Well, you need to tone it down. You look like you're having sex *all* the time. Might be time to act your age." I made a motion of twisting a knob to the left. "Dial it down a little before one of us women in our sexless marriages violently kills you."

"*Match.com*. What can I say? Only one click away."

"One click and a divorce away."

Erica turned toward me. "How is the dream killer, anyway? Still a hard 'no' on the bed-and-breakfast?"

"There's no more discussion. He didn't even leave room to revisit the topic."

"The dream killer strikes again!"

You can see why Rory didn't like her. Because she sure as hell didn't like him.

I said, "I am working on chickens, though."

Erica rolled her eyes. "You've been talking about chickens for forever."

"You know how he is. I have to ease him into these big decisions."

"Big decisions? Getting a few hens is a big decision? I wouldn't even ask him. Find a carpenter—might as well get a cute one—tell him what you want, and while he builds the coop, go find some hens."

I wanted to say thinking like that was why she was divorced, but, not only was that not true, my words would have been plain rude. We don't have boundaries, but we tried to respect each other.

"He thinks I couldn't handle them dying," I admitted.

Erica cocked her head. "He has a point there."

"Yeah, but I'll figure it out. You can't live if you let the fear of death stand in the way."

"Oh, I didn't know I was speaking with my other friend, Plato." In a higher voice, she asked, "Mrs. Philosopher, have you seen Margot? She was here a minute ago. The very tiny woman with First Lady hair who eats air now."

I laughed and said, "Funny. You're hilarious."

She continued, "If you can convince him to see a couple's therapist with you, you might win some of your battles. You can't give him whatever he wants and not get anything in return." Erica was ignorant of my pressure-cooking salvation, which is good evidence that a big part of me knew how crazy I was being.

I said, "I know, I know. I don't want to nag him about therapy yet. We're getting better."

"Are you? Are you really, Margot? Getting better?"

"Sort of."

"Sort of isn't good enough for my best friend. You deserve so much better than Rory Simpson. You deserve better than I have. You're such a catch. That's why I don't want you hanging around my new husband. He'll see what he *could* have gotten."

"Oh, hush," I said. "You're *such* a catch."

She fluttered her eyes. "I am, aren't I? Please, keep going. Tell me more."

I looked at the Vietnamese women working on us and wondered how much they could understand. They knew some English, and I could only assume they'd been listening and comprehending most of what we'd been saying for years. Needless to say, I appreciated their discretion.

The cheap wine flowed as the technicians finished our feet and started on our fingers. Erica and I laughed with each other until both our eyes were full of tears. I don't know what I would have done without her.

I eventually told her about my latest episode with the dream killer. I said, "I touched his ding-dong last night."

Erica's jaw dropped. "The dream killer has a ding-dong?"

I cracked up. "Believe it or not."

Wrinkling her nose, she asked, "What does it do? Does it move?"

"He pushed me away."

Erica raised her voice. "Margot Simpson, if you don't get a handle on this marriage, I will disown you. Seriously."

"Hold your voice down," I said, looking at the woman a few chairs down. She was reading a magazine, but she might be able to overhear our conversation if we weren't careful. I said, "Please don't tell the whole world. He is a public figure."

Erica lowered her voice. "You touched him, and he pushed

you away? I'll tell you right now. He's either batting for the other team, or he's running around on you. Actually, maybe he's batting for the other team *and* running around on you. You need to watch how he looks at other men. Look at you, Margot. You're so hot even I could go after you, and I'm a long way from being a lesbian. Anyway, what was he *thinking*?"

"He's distracted, that's all. You know, this talk of running for the senate."

"Don't you follow the headlines? Politicians love sex. All of them. If they're not getting it from their wives, they're getting it somewhere else."

I turned toward her. "Oh, don't be silly. Rory?"

Erica nodded her head. "Yes, Rory. Believe it or not, there are women out there who crave being with someone in power. They want the mayor slash dream killer inside their bodies. They don't care that he's a selfish imbecile."

"Okay, okay. Settle down. He *is* my husband."

"I'm sorry, Margot, but I'm serious. You need to hire a private investigator. Just see what's going on. Unless he's decided he likes men, there's something going on. Men need sex. That's it, period. End of story."

"It's not always as simple as that. I don't even think he can get it up most of the time. I'm telling you, sex is not even on his mind. For him, sex is cleaning out his inbox. Sex is finding his next vote."

"I hope you're right, Margot, but I don't think men have changed since the beginning of time. I bet Adam cheated on Eve."

"They were the only two people on earth back then."

"Then Adam was screwing a donkey. Trust me."

I shook my head. How do you tell your best friend that in a real marriage you know what's going on with your partner at all times? Her last marriage wasn't like mine with Rory. They had real issues. They weren't even right for each other. Rory and I were destined to be together, and despite our current situation, we were deeply connected. I knew what was going on with him. Yes, many men since the beginning of time have craved sex. But plenty of men simply crave power.

Rory craved power.

6

I TAKE HIM LUNCH

If you know what a man wants, you can make him love you. That was my reasoning, anyway. If Rory craved power, I'd give it to him.

Erica and I finished up at the salon and then pushed our carts through Target and Marshall's together. I spent a little more money than I should have, and so did Erica. It's not my fault that the two stores had such cute things on sale. We would typically grab lunch, but Erica was going to dine with her husband. She invited me to join them, but in my current state of sex and food deprivation, that's the last thing I wanted to do. When you're down and out, and your marriage is struggling, you sure as heck don't want to go sit at a table with two flirting lovebirds desperately trying to keep their clothes on throughout the meal. Besides, I didn't eat these days, so what was I going to do?

I drove along Main Street toward South Willard, driving carefully over the gray slush. It must have been a few degrees over freezing, as the snow on the trees was slowly turning to water and dripping to the ground. Passing by the University of Vermont, I saw Rory's favorite taco truck with a line starting to form at the window. Perhaps my gift of power today would be to deliver lunch to my hardworking husband. I tried to call him, but the call went to voicemail. He ate later than the more regular noon hour, so I wasn't worried that he'd already eaten. It's the thought that counts, anyway. On the chance my timing was off for Rory, I could always give the tacos to the young and beautiful Kim. Maybe I'd slip a little rat poison in there. Just kidding. Sort of. Maybe sprinkle a laxative? Nothing lethal. Even I have boundaries. I'm not a killer, for goodness' sake. Not yet.

I found a parking spot nearby, pulled on my coat, and left the warmth of my car. The icy winds from Lake Champlain cut through the air, and I tightened my scarf as I dashed across the street to take a place in line at the taco truck.

As a vegetarian, I prefer never to buy meat, but I was about to make an exception. This was part of the power I'd give Rory today. In an effort to please him, I'd reluctantly compromise my beliefs. Through chattering teeth, I ordered one *lingua*, one *chorizo*, and one *carne* taco. I didn't want to know what went into making those things, and I tried not to think about the animals that had been sacrificed for my husband's brief lunchtime joy.

Driving into the heart of downtown, I slowed to enjoy the Christmas decorations. Lights covered the trees on either side of Church Street. The lampposts were dressed in red and white to look like candy canes. People wearing heavy jackets and ski hats dashed in and out of stores, many probably looking for last-minute gifts. I finally parked and went to find my husband.

I held onto the railing as I carefully climbed the stone steps of City Hall. As I made my way toward Rory's upstairs office, I stopped to visit with several people, wishing them happy holidays and asking about their families. I worried the tacos would be cold by the time I reached Rory, but it was better to deliver cold tacos than for me to come off as being anything less than darling Margot to his coworkers.

Nadine, the one I liked to hide with at parties, was sitting at her desk. A picture of the president hung behind her on the wall. She looked past her computer screen and said, "Hey, girl. What are you doing here?"

"I thought I'd bring the—" I almost called him the dream killer but caught myself. "I brought my sweet babycakes lunch. Is he here?"

Nadine grinned. "Yep, he's in the office."

I started toward the door, thinking of cold tacos. "I'm sure he's on the phone, but I'm going in anyway."

"You can do whatever you want. We all know you're the boss." After we shared a smile, she returned her eyes to the screen.

I knocked and pushed open the door. Rory was standing over a patch of fake turf in the middle of the office with a putter in his hand. As he spoke through a headset to someone on the other end, he tapped a golf ball toward a hole. I'd given him that toy and was glad to see him using it.

"There's no way they will give you a permit," Rory said and then listened patiently. My husband turned toward me and smiled, then quickly returned to his phone conversation. "Yes, I'm fully aware that I'm the mayor, but there's nothing I can do about it, Wesley. I live by the same laws we all do."

Adding to my loving gestures for the morning, I pulled the tacos out of the white bag, unwrapped them from the foil, and arranged them neatly next to his keyboard. I'd even remembered to ask for a to-go cup of his favorite green hot sauce. I sat in one of the chairs by his desk and waited for him to finish the call. As I always did while waiting for him in that chair, I enjoyed the framed photographs on the wall. Other than one of his parents, they were all pictures of Jasper and me. My favorite was the one of Jasper standing to applause after winning one of his first recitals when he was only three. Three, I say! I couldn't help but beam with pride. There was one of me on stage in a production of *The Sound of Music* from when I was in my early twenties, a time that felt no closer than the Ice Age. There were a few shots of the three of us in different countries on our family trips. Skiing in Chamonix, exploring Rory's roots in Glasgow, and chasing the northern lights while in Finland.

I wondered if he ever looked at these pictures. I wondered if he felt like I did when I strolled down memory lane. When I saw these pictures, I craved making more memories just like these. Did he even see the pictures anymore, or were they solely there to enhance his image as a family man? Had someone on his team suggested hanging the pictures? Hopefully, they were displayed for both reasons. We'd had such fun together traveling back then. That's when Jasper and I'd been able to pull Rory away from work and get him to cut loose.

Rory ended his call and set the putter against the wall. "What are you doing here?" he asked. And then he added, almost like he had to, "What a nice surprise."

Was it, Rory? Was it a nice surprise? I pointed at his desk and said, "I brought you tacos."

He hadn't noticed them yet. "Oh, wow. Thanks."

"You don't seem too excited."

He touched his belly. "I have a business lunch in like five minutes, and I'm already feeling fat."

"Just eat one. I didn't know you had a lunch. I'm sorry."

"Don't be sorry. I appreciate the gesture."

The *gesture*? Who talks like that? I could see he was not only surprised but disturbed by my visit. I stood abruptly and gathered the tacos. "I'll take these home. You can heat them up later."

"Oh, c'mon, Marge."

"Please don't call me Marge."

"I know, I'm sorry. I am appreciative, I just... I wish you'd called."

I looked at the floor. "I did."

Rory walked around the desk. "I wish I'd known you were coming, that's all." He touched my arm. "Today is tough for me."

I sat back in the chair. "Can we sit together for five minutes?" I wanted him to ask how my day was going, what I was thinking about. I wanted to wave my hands in the air and say, "I'm here! I'm here! I'm trying to show you how much I love you. I'm trying with every fiber of my being to be a great wife."

He shook his head. "Not today. Please understand. I have five guys waiting for me at Leunig's. Can we talk later?"

I had a feeling that if it hadn't been five guys waiting at Leunig's, there would have been something else. I was an intruder. I put on a smile that gave no indication I was upset. I stood and said lightheartedly, "I knew I was taking a gamble. It was worth a shot. At least we were able to spend a moment together." I pecked him on the cheek. "Go tear up your day."

"Are you mad at me?" He offered his finest smile.

I forced an even brighter smile. "Not in the least. We committed to all this hard work together. I just wanted to show you that I love you."

"Message received, loud and clear." Another kiss, and he nearly ran out the door. I'd forgotten until now, but his mismatched socks were the last thing I saw.

~

I LEFT IN A SAD HAZE. Rather than going home, I decided my earlier Target- and Marshall's-fueled retail therapy hadn't been enough. For me, no true retail therapy session is complete without a stop at Williams-Sonoma. By stop, I mean setting up a temporary residency. I could never just swing by my favorite store. When I walked through those doors, I came to play.

I don't even want to tell you the truth, but oh, well. As I strolled into the store, two of the ladies in green aprons waved and one of them said, "Welcome back, Margot."

I smiled and said, "Hi, Alicia. Hi, Beth. How are you?"

Alicia, to my knowledge the newest and youngest employee at the store, said, "Let us know if we can help you find anything." She waved a hand at me and grinned. "But I think you know your way around."

Like any good shopper, something came alive in my eyes when I worked my way through the store. I could scan two displays simultaneously, looking for both new items and any discounts worth checking out. Seeing all these kitchen gadgets immediately made me feel better.

The first thing I focused on was an Instant Pot. A newer version and one that had a larger capacity than the pressure cooker I already had. Considering my whole plan to fix my marriage revolved around an Instant Pot, I felt like I should have the best. I carried the box toward the checkout and started my stack. Then there was a juicer. Did I already have one? Yes. Was it this nice? No. Did it join my stack? Yes, indeed. I added two new spatulas, an adorable pair of reindeer oven mitts, and a set of Christmas bistro towels. As the pile by the register grew, so did my heart, and all my troubles dissolved, at least for a brief moment. I bought such a large load that Alicia helped me out to my car after checking out.

By the time I returned home, I felt only a little better. I swear, a visit to Williams-Sonoma could have fixed all my woes a couple of months ago. Now it was only a part of the remedy. What next? Fortunately, I never ran out of ideas, but I needed to clean the house first.

After washing, setting up, and playing with all my new toys —and disposing of the bags, packaging, and receipts—I began cleaning the house. I slipped a few pressure releases into the cleaning downstairs. I stuck a giant ball of hair and dust into the top drawer of the dream killer's desk. I rearranged a few of the books, which originally had been lined up alphabetically on the shelf. Little things to make me happy. Totally harmless!

Accomplishing as much as I could in one day, I finished with the bathrooms. With Philippe following behind, I hiked the stairs wearing yellow rubber gloves. I polished the clawfoot tub and the sinks. As I knelt to clean the toilet, the final urge to satisfy my current depression hit me like a witch swinging her broom across my head. I'd thought about this one before but had never acted upon the idea. I slowly twisted my head toward Rory's sink and saw his blue toothbrush. A smile rushed over me. Thank God no one was filming me, because I must have looked like the most conniving and deranged wife on earth. I removed his toothbrush from the holder and returned to the toilet.

Was I really going to do this?

Apparently.

I lifted the lid and sprayed an organic solution around the rim. I raised my arm, looked at his clean toothbrush one more time, and reached into the bowl. I felt so guilty. I stopped with the bristles an inch away from the porcelain. It wasn't the dirtiest toilet bowl in the world, but it needed cleaning. Using his toothbrush would cross a line.

Was that what saving this marriage would take?

No. I couldn't do it. I shook my head, repulsed that I'd even considered the notion. I stood to return the brush to its holder. At the last second though, I changed my mind yet again. Yes, saving this marriage would require sacrifice. He'd gotten the wife of a lifetime, and the only thing he had to do was brush his teeth with a dirty toothbrush!

I returned to the toilet, and without another thought—at least without another doubt—I began scrubbing. Nothing could have wiped the grin off my face. By the time I was done with that toilet, you could have had Christmas Eve dinner on it.

Rory's toothbrush, on the other hand. Repulsive.

As I finished, I fell onto my butt, cackling. Deranged Margot strikes again. Rory probably thought he had complete control over me. Little did he know this entire year had been my game. *My* game. *My* plan.

To be fair, I did run his toothbrush under hot water for a minute after I finished. I'm not a complete witch. Well, honestly, it wasn't a whole minute. I ran the brush under luke-warm water for few seconds though. Such a witch!

Was I losing my mind or what?

Say what you will, but I felt better. So much better, as if my chest were finally opening up and my brow unfurrowing. I felt so great, in fact, that I felt like cooking. I went downstairs and began flipping through cookbooks.

As I reached to pick up a second book, Rory called. He said, "I'm so sorry about earlier. You were so sweet to bring me tacos. I can't wait to eat them for breakfast."

"Seriously, darling, it hasn't crossed my mind since. No big deal." I didn't care anymore, though saying it hadn't crossed my mind was a stretch. I added, "I was just trying to brighten your day."

"You did that," he said. "And it's great for everyone in City Hall to see how much you care."

I bit my tongue. Couldn't he leave politics out of it for once? Was our entire life about public image? He trucked on. "Still, I want you to know how much I appreciate you. Why don't we do something special tonight? We could go out. Or I could bring home a great bottle of wine, and we could listen to music. Jasper is gone, so we could have a romantic evening—just the two of us. If you feel like cooking, I'm all in. Or I could bring something home. We can do delivery. I don't mean to ask you on a date and then beg you to cook."

"I don't mind cooking." The truth was, a big bright smile lifted my face. He had not asked me on such a date in eons. I said, "I'd love to cook. Is there anything you're dying for?"

"I wouldn't know where to begin." After a pause, he said, "Italian? Your Bolognese?"

My mouth watered. "You're on. I think I have everything. You want homemade pasta?"

"Only if you feel like it."

I whispered, "Anything for you."

"I can hardly wait. I'll leave as soon as possible."

Oh, my gosh, I felt so happy. I ran around the kitchen pulling out ingredients. If he wanted a date, I would give him a date he'd never forget. I told you, I wasn't far from waking him up from his dream.

When you've been cooking as long as I have, you know that timing is everything. So before I did anything else, I raised my sauce to a simmer on the stove. Then I flew up the stairs and picked through my underwear drawer. Only the finest and sexiest for the mayor of Burlington tonight. Yes, I thought, if he wanted a date, I'd be ready to give him one he'd never forget.

Thankfully, I remembered to replace his tainted toothbrush with a new one from under the sink before I returned to the kitchen.

I anticipated a kiss tonight.

7

I COOK HIM DINNER

By the time Rory walked through the door, the mouthwatering scents of basil, tomatoes, and oregano wafted through our sparkling-clean house. If I do say so myself, I looked stunning in my rather revealing black dress with spaghetti straps. The cut was so low my boobs might as well have been hanging out. My back was exposed, and my dress barely covered my bottom. I don't even know why I'd bought this thing, but it felt apropos for tonight. You know, spaghetti straps and spaghetti. I hoped Rory would make the correlation, and his hunger wouldn't stop with a clean plate, if you know what I mean. Dessert, love?

One thing I'd learned the hard way—scratch that—the easy way, was that when you get a new body, you need new clothes. You think I'd gone crazy at Williams-Sonoma? Let me tell you what. Not only were every employee at Nordstrom and Neiman Marcus and I on a first-name basis, I even knew the names of the women who worked in the parking garage. To be on the safe side, I'd packed up all my "fat" clothes and stored them in the garage, just in case I ever fell apart. For now, in my bedroom, there wasn't a trace of my old body. It was the new, slender Margot all the way.

My loving husband walked into the house and did the exact opposite of what he usually did. Typically, he walked through the door, muttered a "hello," and went straight to his office to plug in and finish the day. A few more phone calls, emails, and articles. I, by then, being the dutiful housewife, would have sorted the mail and left his stack on his desk. Only after he'd finished with all of the above would he come find me.

To my delight, not today! I heard his bag drop at the side door, and he waltzed into the kitchen. "Look at you! Wow!"

I beamed. "Your workday ends now." I turned to him, and he kissed me on the mouth. I couldn't believe it. "What's gotten into you?" I whispered, fingering his collar.

"You have. Look at you. I don't even know if I can wait until dessert."

The dress was working! I said, "Now, you're talking."

Rory grabbed my waist and kissed my mouth and neck. He felt my breasts for a moment, and his touch tingled my entire body. I came alive in parts that had nearly been mummified.

I pushed him away and told him the sauce would burn. He dropped his head and said reluctantly, "We can't have that, can we?"

As I went to stir the Bolognese, and the aroma thickened in the air, he groaned hungrily. Everything in our world had come together. I couldn't believe it, and I'd never been so excited about a date in my entire life. I felt like a bad guy in a stupid cartoon when he says with steepled hands, "My plan is coming together."

Rory asked about my day. Wait. Stop. Yep, you read that right! He asked about my day! We could have stopped there, and he already would have won. I told him about the nail salon and that I'd picked up a thing or two at Williams-Sonoma, "thing or two" being a loose phrase. Who cared about details, anyway? A thing, two things. Thirty things. Just numbers.

Anyway, rather than casting another countless critical jab at Erica, he took my hand and looked at my red nails. I'd been getting my nails done at the same salon for years, and he'd never once taken my hand and checked my nails. What had gotten into this guy?

"They're really pretty," he said. His compliment actually sounded sincere, like he couldn't believe that he hadn't noticed how nice my nails were before. He backed up and looked at my feet. I was wearing delicious red, pointy-toe stiletto mules, and I modeled my legs and feet for him like he was window shopping. He gave me another compliment, and I swear, I remember thinking I couldn't handle many more. He'd buttered me up so well, he could have asked me for anything in the world at that moment, and I would have said, "Yes!"

How about a threesome?

Why not four?

Do you mind if I take a week off and go with the guys to Canada to watch hockey?

Do I mind? Of course not! Take two weeks!

Do you mind doing the dishes?

Not at all! I don't want you doing the dishes, Rory. You've worked too hard already today.

You get the picture.

Rory went upstairs to change while I set the table. He played Van Morrison and uncorked a left-bank Bordeaux, which is a merlot-based wine from my favorite wine region. We raised our glasses and toasted to falling in love all over again.

As if he couldn't have laid it on any thicker, he asked, "Is there anything I can do to help?"

I nearly dropped my glass. That was a question I hadn't heard since Jasper was in diapers. "Why, yes, I'm sure," I said, trying to think of something. Anything. When an idea surfaced, I said, "Why don't you make your delicious garlic bread?"

"I'd be happy to."

Was this happening? Is this how all marriages come back together? A year of hard work and then one day it's back? Just like it hadn't been lost? Here we are. Right where we started. I was in such a happy fog, I didn't dare consider any other alternative than the truth: I'd shown him how to love again.

So often those days we'd eaten at the island or in front of the television in the living room. Not tonight. We sat at the dining-room table facing each other. Rory dimmed the lights on the chandelier and lit two tall white candles that flickered light between us. We didn't even once talk about his work or his projected career path. He asked me questions, and I happily answered. And then I asked him questions, just like you do when you're in the earlier stages of a relationship. No questions about work, but about hockey and where he wanted to travel next. What he and Jasper might do over the holidays for a little father-son time. So many times lately, our conversations had been difficult. Not tonight. We were reconnecting like lovers who'd been torn apart by war.

After dinner, he suggested a Skype session with Jasper. I texted our son and gave him a heads up, and when he rang us, Rory and I scooted our chairs together. We squeezed our heads into the screen and said, "Hi." Jasper must have thought we were drunk. It had been a while since he'd seen us beaming so.

To have Jasper in on this wonderful night was a dream come true. We talked about his music camp for a while, and then he said something about considering a Texas school for college so he could be near a teacher he was studying with. I shut down for a moment. One of the things a mom dreads, in the natural progression of life, is the thought of her child actually leaving home and going off to college.

Collecting myself, I asked him exactly what he'd learned, and Jasper told us about some new scales and chords. Though I was a music major, he'd already far surpassed my understanding of theory. Rory's eyes glazed over whenever Jasper talked with great passion about music. Rory didn't have a musical bone in his body. He loved listening to music, but he had no musical abilities. He played no instruments and couldn't carry a tune if his life depended on it. In fact, I'm surprised Rory's lack of musicality hadn't canceled out the musical genes I'd passed on to Jasper. Somehow, our son had been born a musical genius. I could hardly wait to see where his talent would lead him and where his career path would go. I believed, as all his teachers had assured us, that he would be remembered for his musical contributions long after he was gone. He had that caliber of ability, talent, and drive.

We eventually said goodbye to our son and closed the laptop, and Rory and I did the dishes. Usually I did the dishes alone. Tonight, we were a team. Halfway through, Rory took my hand, and we danced to Van Morrison. He spun me around, and I giggled. He whispered into my ear that he loved me. He pushed me away and looked into my eyes. He put his hand on my waist and pulled me in for a kiss. Not a twenty-years-of-marriage kiss. I'm talking about the real thing. A kiss filled with desire. Not unlike our first ones in New York. I even felt his tongue touch my teeth.

My knees nearly buckled as I thought of how warming it was to have him back.

And it felt like this wasn't a tease. We'd cracked the core of our issues. Tomorrow would be the same. We'd gotten over the hump. Margot and Rory Simpson, the sequel!

As he touched my more sensitive areas, I sensed a momentary hesitation inside me, a lingering hurt from the rejection the night before. I didn't want him to turn me down again, so I let him lead. Even when it's a man you've known for twenty years, the man you've slept with countless times, rejection hurts.

Rory touched my stomach, my flat stomach, the flattest it had been since college. It was the first time he'd touched it since I'd lost all the weight. He was "seeing" me, and it was all I could do to restrain myself. He guided his fingers up to my breasts, which were smaller than ever, but also more perfect. At least I liked them. A wave of lightheadedness ran over me. Rory thrust his tongue into my mouth as he moaned his cravings. I hadn't felt so wanted in many years.

I felt him grow harder as he pressed against me, and for the second time that year—the second time in twenty-four hours—I reached between his legs. He swelled even more in my hand. I gasped, wanting him so badly.

"I've missed you, baby," I whispered.

"You and me both," he admitted. "Where have I been? God, where have I been?"

His words fed my own craving, and I bit his earlobe and pressed my body against him, pulling him closer and closer. Rory moved the straps of my dress off my shoulders, and I shimmied out. He unhooked my bra and kissed my breasts and ran his hands up and down my body, as if he were exploring me for the first time.

"Leave your shoes on, okay?" he asked.

"Okay," I muttered. His fetish was making love to me while I wore sexy shoes. I nodded as I unbuttoned and stripped off his shirt. I lowered my hands and quickly unbuttoned and unzipped his pants. I pulled down his boxer briefs and dropped to my knees. He moaned louder as I took him in my hands and mouth.

He soon lifted me up onto the counter, and we clumsily attempted to make love. We couldn't quite make it work. That was okay, though. We both laughed at the folly as he led me onto the couch in the next room. Rory and I made the finest love I could ever have imagined. As we danced together sexually, I bathed in the joy of having him back. No longer would I need to fear going at this world alone. Everything would be all right.

It wasn't until later, while we cuddled on the couch, that he asked, "Did you intentionally mismatch my socks? I went to work with one black and one navy today. Didn't even realize it until Nadine mentioned it."

I smiled. *Busted.* I almost denied it, but that would be no way to start our reunion. "Guilty as charged."

"You're going after me right now, aren't you? Am I driving you crazy or what?"

"I've...I've been frustrated, my love. That's all."

"I can tell. Mismatched socks. Letting Phil up on the bed. Deleting my games. God knows what else." He stroked my hair. "I love you. Today as much as ever."

"I know you do," I said. "I need you to show it more. You can tell me all day, and it doesn't make a difference. I know you have your aspirations, and I fully support you, but we still need to have a marriage."

He glided his fingers along my forehead and kissed my cheek. "You're right, baby. You're right."

"By the way, why was Nadine looking at your ankles?"

"Oh, c'mon."

"I'm just kidding."

We cleaned up the kitchen and met in bed an hour later. Philippe walked in circles on his bed and eventually settled into his spot. Rory grabbed the remote and pointed it at the TV. I reached for my book. Rory stopped before pressing the button and put down the remote. He turned and said, "Let's read out loud to each other. You choose the book. We always say we're going to do it but never do. Enough talk."

I looked with eager, yet skeptical, eyes. "Rory Simpson, who are you?"

My husband shrugged his shoulders and said, "A man in love."

We spent the next twenty minutes reading one of the new bestsellers to each other. I loved hearing his voice, but I had to work hard to follow the story. I couldn't stop thinking about how much effort I'd put into saving us. He'd been daydreaming his life away and forgotten I was there. As opposed to me turning into the ultimate nagging bitch this past year, the wife who screams and complains that her husband doesn't "see" her, I'd taken the counterintuitive approach. Sometimes, that kind of approach works. Rather than kicking and screaming and going on the offensive, I'd done what Jesus might have done. If he steals my coat, I give him my shirt. I'd covered Rory with love, and that love had brought him back to the light. Sure, we'd have setbacks. I wasn't an idiot caught in illusions. I wasn't alone in my daydream. But we would be okay. We'd taken the first giant leap and had rediscovered the magic, and I was pretty proud of myself for making it happen.

I couldn't let the night go without taking advantage of his mood. I said to him, "Honey, I know this drives you crazy, and I know it makes little sense to you, but I need to ask something of you. It would mean so much to me." He stifled a yawn and encouraged me to tell him.

I let it out. "Before you say no, please hear me out. I guess you always do that...but really hear me out with an open mind. Actually, consider my proposal. Yes, you agreed to let me adopt Philippe, and that was awesome. I'm so happy to have him. He makes me extremely happy. But understand, my whole life has been about animals. I'm a vegetarian because I love animals. What is so wrong with having animals around our house? It's not like I'm asking to have a horse. I understand that starting a bed-and-breakfast is too much right now. Maybe it can eventually work out, though. For now, all I'm asking for are three or four chickens. I will build the coop myself if you're worried about it."

He turned onto his side, and with the kindest, warmest eyes I've ever seen, he said, "How about we build the coop together?"

And we lived happily ever after.

The end.

Or so I hoped.

8

A PUBLIC LIFE

D o you remember the first time you fell in love? It might have been when you were fifteen. He clumsily asked you to a movie. Halfway through the opening credits, he reached for your hand. A week later you kissed. Your whole world was turned upside down.

Maybe Cupid found you with his arrow much later. For some it happens in college. Perhaps you hadn't met the right guy in high school, but in your freshman year, you met a boy at a party. He was looking to hook up like the rest of them, but something was different about him. He took you to see a school play. You studied together. You walked hand in hand through the halls, and you couldn't get enough of each other. Everything started to make sense.

He was all you could think about. Everything around you glittered. You were walking chill bumps. The days shimmered brighter. Music touched you deeper. Even the way you woke up was different. You tasted something almost divine.

This morning, my eyes popped open, and the world was beautiful. I was in love, all over again.

Rory woke me with a kiss and squeezed my bottom. I giggled as he climbed out of bed and into the shower. I patted the bed, and Philippe hopped up to join me. I pulled him close and told him that today would be our best day in many years. I told him we'd go to the doggy bakery, and he wagged his tail. He didn't know what I was saying, but he knew today was going to be all right. That was for sure.

I trotted into the bathroom. Rory was humming, which would have sounded awful to anyone other than the one who loved him. I had no idea what he was humming, and the notes he attempted weren't even notes. But gosh, did he sound good to my lovestruck ears. I checked the rack to make sure he had a fresh towel. I even went to the drawer in his closet and matched up the rest of the mismatched socks.

There was only one thing I wanted to do for myself today. When my soul soared like it was doing today, I wanted to be in the kitchen. Now that I had someone to cook for—someone who *deserved* my cooking—I could barely contain my culinary urge. The excitement nearly pushed me down the stairs. In another rare twist, I decided that not only would I celebrate our reunion—or, as I thought of it, Rory's reawakening—I would also celebrate the year of culinary torture I'd endured by breaking away from my diet. For one day only, I'd let myself go.

As I weighed out flour for my first recipe, Rory entered the kitchen in a pinstriped suit. We kissed on the mouth, I wished him a good day, and I watched him drive away. My heart had never felt so full.

The sweets came first. I made blondies and eclairs, two of my favorite desserts. Then I tackled some savory treats, including Rory's favorite, a simple snack mix made with Amish butter and vegan Worcestershire sauce. If he didn't eat it all when he returned home, I'd bag some up for friends and family. I almost had a handful but was afraid of completely losing control.

Once the ovens were full and every burner on the stove occupied, I considered dinner. I flipped through a few cookbooks for ideas and decided on a vegetarian cassoulet, a perfect winter meal. While singing along with a radio station playing show tunes, I went to work. I took a break every once in a while to reach out to a few friends and family. Along with being a bit of a mess the past year, I'd nearly alienated myself. I texted Jasper first, just to tell him I loved him. I called my parents in Virginia; I even invited them to visit! I called Erica and talked to her for forever; she was excited for me. I said, "Told you so!"

"Yeah, yeah, yeah," she said back, but she didn't sound convinced. I knew she wanted me to be happy, but for some reason, it was hard for her to trust Rory.

I was in such a jolly mood I even called a few friends from college with whom I hadn't been in contact for more than a year.

After a well-deserved nap cuddling with Philippe, I went down to admire my work. You should have seen the eclairs. I picked up one of those stunning creations and admired this piece of art. In my earlier baking years, I would have rolled out a green fondant icing and used a holly cutter to make three holly leaves. I would have put the leaves together on top of white icing, then squeezed three dots of red icing at the base of the holly leaves. As I became a more experienced chef, I learned how to use healthier ingredients and stopped using food dyes. To replace the green fondant hollies, I used mint leaves. Rather than the dots of red icing, I used pomegranate seeds. I know, I know. I'm brilliant.

I couldn't bring myself to eat the beautiful pastries. The slippery slope of breaking my diet scared the heck out of me. Oh, well. Feeling skinny might just be better than enjoying good food. My confidence slipped for a moment. What if I did gain weight? What if I grew my hair back out? Would Rory and I have to relive all those hard times?

Steering away from troubling mental waters, I told myself that it wasn't just my new body and haircut that had gotten Rory back. Ultimately, it was the love I'd shown, the love I'd refused to let go.

Still, I couldn't bring myself to indulge.

I texted Rory and told him about dinner tonight. I hoped he'd text me right back, but no such luck. I rationalized that I couldn't expect that suddenly he'd be free all the time and waiting to instantaneously return my every text.

With time to spare, I climbed the stairs to our cozy sitting room, where I liked to watch the news while I ironed. To some, I might sound like such a boring housewife, but I enjoyed ironing, and for me, nothing was boring about being a housewife. It was one of my greatest callings and one of my greatest challenges. Call me old-fashioned, and you'd be spot-on. I loved being a housewife and homemaker, especially when my efforts were appreciated.

I collected a few articles of clothing out of the dryer and a handful of shirts from Rory's closet. Each of those shirts had my little trademark crease in the back collar. I thought I'd better iron those out now that life was back to normal. I didn't want him thinking I still held a grudge. I was almost dancing as I set up the ironing board and started on his first shirt. A supercomfy shag rug covered the hardwood floor, and I loved to squish my toes into it as I worked.

The news on the screen hanging on the wall, much to my

delight, mirrored my joy. Rather than the typical crime or theft or murder, the first piece I caught was about a young Girl Scout who'd been doing card tricks for the elderly at a nearby retirement home. "Bless her heart," I said. Then a piece ran about a dog that had been missing for three months and finally returned home. I looked down at Philippe. "Don't you ever go anywhere, sweetie." Raw tears dripped down my cheeks. What a lovely world we live in.

It goes to show you, when you see what you want and you go after it, you can get it. I saw what was wrong with our marriage. I saw that my partner needed me. And that's what I did, I showed up for him. That's what love is.

As I grabbed the last shirt and ironed the last mischievous crease, a breaking news alert flashed along the bottom of the screen. The text that followed hit me like someone had taken a baseball bat and struck me in the chest.

Rory Simpson infidelity caught on tape!

The breath ran from my lungs as my chest imploded. The iron fell from my hand. I barely heard it drop onto the shaggy rug. I stared, dumbfounded, at the TV and listened to the reporter. "Burlington Mayor Rory Simpson has been discovered in his car, committing sexual acts with a woman who is not his wife."

My phone buzzed and dinged.

The reporter on the television warned of graphic images, just before an enlarged image splashed all over the TV screen. There he was, sitting in his car, and he wasn't alone.

My husband, Rory Simpson.

The mayor of Burlington, Vermont.

The dream killer.

The editors had blurred out his crotch, but the amateur video showed Rory in the front seat of his sedan with a topless woman performing oral sex on him. I didn't recognize her at first. All I could see was a brunette facedown in my husband's lap. He was leaned back on the reclined seat with his eyes closed, and his lips were moving enough that it was obvious he was mumbling something. What was he mumbling? Instructions? Encouragement? Gratitude? He held one hand on the brunette's back.

Bile crept up into my throat.

The woman raised her head. It was Nadine.

Rory smiled as he pulled her up toward him, leaned forward, and almost as if rewarding her for a blow job well done, he kissed her blurred-out breasts. I couldn't believe such an explicit video had been so quickly released for public scrutiny. Released before I had been forewarned. Released before I could contact my son. Released before my whole world fell apart. And, where was Rory in all this? He must have known about the video. I wasn't watching it live, for God's sake. I was sure this incident had happened at least a day before. Why had he not told me before the damned video went public? Why had he come to me last night and tried to make me believe I was the most important thing in his life? Why? Why? Why?

A desperate cry escaped from my lips, and my face felt like it was melting. "No," I whispered. How could he? How could she?

My phone lit up again. And again. Philippe barked.

I grasped the ironing board to steady myself before my legs gave out from under me. Could this be happening? A burning smell crept into my nostrils, and I looked down to find the rug on fire. "Nooooo!" I screamed. The red-hot iron was on its side and had burned a hole through the rug, all the way to the floor. Smoke filled the room as the flames spread. I wasn't wearing shoes, so I couldn't stomp out the fire. Screaming desperately, I grabbed a pillow from the chair and tried to smother the flames. The pillow caught fire.

With Philippe chasing after me, I ran down the stairs and searched frantically for the fire extinguisher. You always intend to keep the extinguisher where you can find it easily, but let's face it, you never expect to need it. If I'd been any less sane, I might not have cared if the house burned down, but it was almost like the burning rug had distracted me and given me a new mission. I forgot about Rory and Nadine for a moment.

Running back up the stairs, I examined the extinguisher. Considering I hadn't immediately known where to find it, I'd certainly never used it before. Who has? I tore the plastic safety tie and pulled the black trigger, spraying white foam all over the room, covering the expensive rug, the floors, the chairs. I dropped the extinguisher and unplugged the iron. I fell onto my knees with a pounding heart. The white foam surrounded my legs. I was trembling like I'd been pulled out of icy waters.

I don't remember the next few minutes. I don't think I cried. I wasn't that together. I think I'd gone numb to the point where I'd nearly lost all bodily function. I'd just experienced a couple of real shockers.

But I remember coming to my senses, even as much as twenty minutes later. I was still on my knees, sitting in the foam. My hands shook. My phone rang incessantly, and I slowly forced myself to stand. I'd received twenty-five missed calls and forty text messages. Erica and my parents had called the most.

Jasper's call was the one I'd just missed. I called him back.

"Mom?" he said, and I knew he knew.

I burst into tears and covered my mouth so he wouldn't hear me cry. After a few agonizing seconds, I muttered, "Honey."

"Mom, what's happening?"

How does a mother answer that question with the vulgar

truth? I didn't even understand what was happening, but at that moment, nothing mattered more than Jasper and his security. No matter what I'd seen on television, I had a duty as his mom. I literally bit down hard on my tongue to find some control and then, with the irony taste of blood in my mouth, I said, "I don't know exactly, Jasper."

"Is it true?"

Maybe he hadn't seen the news yet. I said, "Jasper, do not watch the television. I don't know what is true, but I want you to come home. Please do not watch the news. Do not talk to anyone about this. Do you understand?"

"Are you okay, Mom?"

"I don't know. Will you come home, honey? I need you to come home."

"I'll be there as soon as I can."

"I'll make arrangements."

"I can get there, Mom. Don't worry."

"No, please, sweetie. I'll make a couple of phone calls and book you on the first available flight home. I'll get back to you with the info." He finally relented, and we both said, "I love you," as we ended the call.

I dropped the phone, fell back into the thick foam, collapsing onto my back. Philippe waded through the sea of white and licked my face. I pulled him closer.

9

RORY COMES HOME

After making arrangements for Jasper's return, a need for hot water came over me, like soaking in my claw-foot tub might help wash some of this disgusting filth off me—and I'm not talking about the foam. I felt wronged and violated, disrespected and humiliated. Betrayed. I remember walking down the stairs like a zombie, stumbling without motor control, holding onto the walls for balance. I retrieved a bottle of merlot from the bar in the living room and went back upstairs. I entered the bathroom and turned on the hot water, hotter than normal. I thought burning my skin might soften the pain I felt in my heart.

I washed the foam off my body in the shower and then eased into the tub. The water had only risen a couple of inches and hadn't yet warmed the cold porcelain. The hot and cold tore at my flesh. I sat there and stared at the white wall in front of me and felt the steaming water creep up my skin, one inch at a time. Philippe, tapping into his sixth sense, plopped down on the bathmat and watched me with the utmost concern. I sipped the merlot and stared at the blank wall in front of me. The cold sting of the porcelain subsided.

My imagination projected the video onto the wall, and I watched the scene repeatedly, wondering about the truth. It was impossible to deny what had happened, but I could see how the cheating might have occurred. I tried not to blame it on Nadine's big boobs. Of course, I had been going through the same sexual starvation Rory had been, but I hadn't gone out looking for a guy with larger anatomical attributes to satisfy my sexual needs. And Rory's behavior had made it impossible for me to see that he'd needed contact like I had. But I was always —always—there for him. He should have turned to me, not to someone else. If he loved me, that is. It was becoming clear. I should have listened to Erica. Rory was no longer attracted to me, simple as that.

Questions and potential answers swirled like an angry ocean in my seasick mind. How long had this been going on? I thought about the night I had seen Nadine at my house. Had she and my husband already been together? Had this been a yearlong affair or was the revelation of today their first time? She and I got along famously. Was she a calculating bitch inside? Had she been nice to me two nights ago, while secretly thinking about how she enjoyed sleeping with my husband? Had they thought they could fool me? Had they been laughing at me behind my back? I hoped this was their first time. Surely, there was no way a public figure like Rory could have gotten away with infidelity for very long before being caught.

Perhaps even more painful than my husband cheating on me—with a younger woman bursting with Mt. Everest breasts —was the public nature of it all. I'd gotten used to being looked at and stared at by the people of Burlington and even the rest of Vermont. As a couple, Rory and I were kind of a big deal. I was getting used to the idea that I might someday become a senator's wife, which would only increase the public attention we'd endure. But think how this calculated betrayal would affect our family. To think that every person in our city, our state, even the country, had the potential to see that awful video of Nadine going down on my husband—a video that, because it was so explicit, was sure to go viral!

Put me and my feelings aside for a moment—what about Jasper? His friends, classmates, and teachers would be sure to see the video. Once word got around, they'd hunt for it. How was this exposure going to affect Jasper?

Going forward, if Rory's name were entered in a search engine on the internet, the first hits wouldn't be about any great accomplishments in his life, not the fact that he had been an attorney in good standing, not that he'd been elected the mayor of Burlington, not that he was being looked at for a senate position. The first hits would link his name to that video. What a terrible position Rory's action had put us all in—and although Jasper and I had done nothing wrong, we'd be paying the price for Rory's mistake for the rest of our lives. What had he been thinking? Part of me wanted to fly to Texas, find Jasper, and leave the country. Never come back.

I thought of Anthony Weiner and what his wife had gone through. And Bill Clinton and Monica Lewinsky. Elliot Spitzer. All the politicians who'd publicly destroyed their families. How do you survive that? And with Jasper, the son of a public figure, how do you ever forgive your father? How do you walk into the public eye ever again? Everyone would know how bad your life was. No matter how well you lived your own life, that stigma of another family member's wrongdoing would always lurk in the background.

Escaping the projection on the wall, I closed my eyes and

tried to melt away. I still couldn't remove the images. The pleasure exuding from my husband's face. The grimacing and mumbling as Nadine pleasured him. What in the world had he been saying to her?

No matter where my thoughts ran, Rory was there waiting for me like a demon in a horror movie. I wondered what would happen next. He'd called me several times. Would I see him today? Maybe I should leave the house, but where would I go? I felt like the sanctuary of my home might protect me through the coming days. Everyone would see that video. There was nowhere Jasper and I could hide.

I knew that doorbell would soon ring, and I was terrified. Journalists and other vultures would linger for days. Hopefully, we could keep them restricted to the main road. Perhaps the police would help us keep them off our property.

Despite the pain and anger filling my bones, I found it nearly impossible to imagine leaving my husband. I wasn't ready to be on my own. Rory had done most of the banking. Rory had done most of the driving. I had learned to count on him in so many ways. It's not that I couldn't have done those things, but I'd always relied on Rory. Now that I knew I couldn't depend on him, I felt afraid. He was supposed to be our defender. He was my knight in shining armor. At least, he used to be.

I drank more merlot. The burn of the alcohol felt nice. I remember for a moment being distracted by how pleasurable this particular wine was, the exact kind I like: slightly fruity but not overly lush. It reminded me of the Bordeaux Rory and I had drunk the night before, the bottle that had led us to dance and make love. The bottle of merlot-based wine from my favorite region. My thoughts about the wine I was drinking flashed by so quickly amidst my depression that I didn't put it together at the time, but I was drinking from the bottle of merlot from Red Mountain. The bottle of merlot that Nadine had gifted me. It was *that* bottle. Under the circumstances, what irony!

The merlot did its magic, and I drifted into a dream.

~

I WASN'T in the tub anymore.

I was in the kitchen. Waiting for him. It had been three hours since I'd discovered he'd been having an affair with Nadine. I was doing the only thing I knew to do, which was cook. I'd cooked more food than we could eat, but that wasn't stopping me. I wasn't cooking for people to eat. I was cooking to cook, to take my mind off the devastation.

When Rory entered the kitchen, I cut my eyes to him. He dropped his briefcase down onto the tile floor and removed his coat, revealing a pinstriped suit with a red tie underneath. My husband looked at me and sighed. He knew not to step any farther. Not until he had taken the temperature of the room, the temperature of my fury. Not until I'd given him permission. He said, "Darling, I'm sorry. I don't even know how to tell you how sorry I am. I made a big mistake."

"How long have you been sleeping with her?" I spat.

He raised his hands, palms up. "That was the first time."

I thrust my finger at him. "Don't you lie to me."

Talking with his hands, he said, "I swear to you, Margot. It happened. It wasn't even me. You know it wasn't me. I've made the biggest mistake of my life."

"The biggest mistake of your life?" I repeated.

He nodded, like he was already assuming I'd accept his apology.

I said again, "The biggest mistake of your life." I smiled at the absurdity of it all. "You destroyed our family. You just ruined your son's life. You ruined my life. All to get your...ugh!" I clenched both fists.

He stepped toward me. "We can work through this. I know it won't be easy, but please. We can work through this."

"What about last night?" I demanded. "Was that you taking out your sexual feelings for Nadine on me? How could you make love to me like that and then let her suck your cock the next day?"

"It meant nothing," he said. "Honestly."

"You say it didn't," I said, wiping a runaway tear. "And I want to forgive you."

Rory didn't smile, but the optimistic expression on his face indicated that he knew he was winning. That he might actually survive this. That I might not leave him. His smile did something to me inside. My spine straightened with confidence. I turned toward the island and saw the butcher block of knives. I tightened the grip on my right hand and imagined grabbing one of those knives. I looked over and saw the pressure cooker and then the mixer. I saw so many things I could use to hurt him. Everything in my kitchen became a weapon.

There was no way he would leave this kitchen alive. Or at least, there was no way he would leave this kitchen without enduring severe pain. My eyes finally rested on the clay pot in the center of the island that held the spatulas and wooden spoons and other utensils. There was a set of skewers I often used for vegetarian shish kebabs. Without making much of a scene, I reached over and pulled out two skewers, one in each hand. I looked back at him, and the fire in my eyes radiated fury and heat.

His eyes bulged, and his mouth fell agape. He demanded, "What are you doing?"

"You will never cheat on me again."

"No," he promised as his voice cracked. "I won't ever cheat on you again. Please, let's move past this."

I was done talking. I stepped closer to him and whacked him in the head with a skewer. As he raised his hands to protect himself, I hit him in the side with the other one. He screamed in pain. His hands moved each time I struck him, and with each strike, I hit harder and harder. I landed a good clean hit against his cheek, and a red line appeared on his skin.

As his hands flew up to block another stroke, I noticed his unprotected belly. I jabbed the skewer into his skin. He screamed, and as he cowered in pain, I stuck him with the other skewer. Blood stained his blue shirt. I stuck him three more times, and he fell to the ground and shrank into the fetal position. I changed the position of my hands so I could stab him overhanded. Like I was pricking dough, I thrust my fists back and forth, sticking him over and over. I yelled that he would never cheat on me again. How could he ever do this to our family, to Jasper? He swore that it would be the last time as I stabbed him over and over, and blood stained his clothes.

∾

Footsteps ascending the stairs pulled me from my daydream. It took me a moment to realize where I was. I was trembling again. Sweat was dripping into my eyes and down my cheeks. I let out an audible sigh and tried to collect myself. I truly was in a state of shock. This wasn't going to be easy.

Philippe rose to his feet and licked my arm.

I tried to smile at him. He needed to know I was okay. *No, honey. I'm not.*

Rory entered the bathroom. I wished that I'd left the house.

As he stood there looking at me, I felt a brief moment of gratitude that he was alive. That the violence of the last few minutes
had only been in a dream. My eyes went straight to his stomach, to his shirt. There was no blood. I was thankful that I
hadn't hurt him.

It's funny, in a sad way. Rory and I had been married for a
long time, and it almost felt like even an affair couldn't stand in
the way of how we felt about each other. Even if I hated him
with everything I had, I still loved him harder and more than
anyone I'd ever loved. During a marriage of twenty years, we'd
become one with each other. No matter what he'd done to me,
we'd always be one. At least, that's what I wanted to believe.

Much like the daydream I'd had, Rory stood at the door and
didn't dare walk farther in. It's crazy how someone who thinks
he's getting away with something can act so normal, and even
be cocky at times, while continuing his bad behavior—but after
he's been caught, the cockiness is sucked right out of him, and
he looks ashamed. Ashamed because he had been behaving
badly, or ashamed because he hadn't been crafty enough not to
get caught? Not sure.

Rory's eyes were red from crying. There was a slouch in his
posture that he rarely allowed. His bottom lip quivered. I
turned away and looked back at the white wall. I suddenly felt
exposed, and put my left arm over my breasts. I sank deeper
into the water. I wanted to tell him to go away, to leave. Not to
leave forever, but until I processed what had happened. I still
had no idea what I would do. For now, I wanted to hit pause
and analyze the situation. This definitely wasn't a mistake that a
few minutes in the time-out chair could remedy.

Breaking the unbearable verbal silence, he asked, "Are you
okay? I mean...not about...I mean the sitting room. What
happened?"

"An ironing accident," I said, avoiding eye contact.

He nodded his head, as if he weren't surprised. "I'll clean it up. I'm glad you're okay."

"Please don't. I'll deal with it later."

A long, pregnant pause. I could feel the pulse pounding in my wrists.

Rory made a few unintelligible sounds and said, "I refuse to let today get in the way of our marriage." As if he, alone, possessed the power. What was he thinking? He said, "I made the biggest mistake of my life, and I will fix this." Fix this? He was the one who had broken this, but I wasn't sure he had the necessary tools to fix what he'd broken.

All my tension ran to my jaws. I'd already heard these words in my daydream; I was reliving the nightmare.

He continued, "Nadine means nothing. Please believe me. You are my everything. I want to grow old with you. I made a mistake, that's all."

I shook my head and stung him with my stare. "You'll fix this? You made a mistake? Was that mistake getting caught?"

"Oh, c'mon."

"Are you sure Nadine means nothing to you?" I asked. "Was that what you were mumbling to her while she was going down on you? Cheating on your wife of twenty years is *not* a mistake. It is an epic fuckup that will destroy the three of us. Forget about me! What about your son!"

"I've been calling him ever since the news broke. He won't pick up."

"Why would he ever pick up?" I screamed. "You've destroyed his life. No matter what he does, with or without the piano, he will be known as the son of a disrespectful asshole cheating bastard whose betrayal of his family was plastered all over the news!" My eyes darted around the bathroom looking for a weapon. At that moment, I understood the meaning of temporary insanity.

"I know you can't forgive me right now," he said, moving his hands to the cadence of his voice, "and I will not try to sway you. But please know, I've been craving sex, that's it. This was physical. I don't even know the first thing about that girl. I don't even care. She's a nobody."

"Don't go there. I have been the wife of your dreams lately. I would've happily slept with you every single day of this year. I've been there for you, and I have tried. I have tried so many times. You've kept that damned prick in your pants like there was something wrong with it. Don't even try to say you were starved for some kind of touch. Let's be honest, you were starved for those...those huge tatas and that young mouth around your wretched...thing." I shook my head. "No, I'm not even sure you craved those things. I think your giant ego craved to be fed. Maybe you're just a narcissist and need to believe you're desirable to women you've not already had. You knew you had me. You knew I'd always be there for you. I've approached you with love and desire and have suffered humiliation when you turned me away. No, it wasn't sex you wanted, it was an ego boost, you selfish bastard." I could barely talk but eventually found his eyes and said, "When I look at you now, I see evil. Pure evil!"

"Don't say that," he pleaded. "Please don't say that. I admit I haven't been me lately. Today is the biggest wake-up call of my life. I've been walking around focused on work, focused on this potential senate run. Margot, please understand. I have been focused on my career, and I've been selfish and a jerk..." A jerk? That was the worst thing he could call himself? He paused to battle a sob working its way closer to the surface. In a softer voice he said, "I see that now. Please, you have to understand what it feels like for me right now." He raised his hand in the air as if swearing an oath, his signature move. "I feel like I'm looking at the past year or two or even three and seeing this stranger that inhabited my body. You know that's not me."

I shook my head and sank even lower in the water. "You disgust me. We wouldn't even be having this discussion if you hadn't been caught and exposed! You'd be right out there every day disrespecting your family. Not to mention the families of the ones who were with you. What about Nadine's husband? Did either one of you even think about what you were doing to the people who loved you? If I'd done what you did and a video filled the screen for all to see, would you just disregard it and think nothing of it?"

He pointed at his own chest as he broke down. "This is me. I'm here right now. I'm the man you married. I'm the man who wants to grow old with you. I'm the man who wants to take care of you. Today, our marriage starts over. Our family starts over. One day, we will look back and know that this day and what happened is what saved us."

"Do you actually believe what you're saying? Do you expect me to believe it? Do you believe you can decide on your own that you'll set new rules and that I'll acquiesce and agree to them? Do you actually believe your betrayal could *ever* be considered what saved our marriage when it was the very thing that destroyed it? What in the name of all that's holy are you thinking?"

The shock and absurdity of it all was draining. An overwhelming exhaustion ran over me, dissipating some anger. I didn't know what else to say, and I didn't want to talk about it anymore. Losing myself in the white wall, I fell deep into thought. I couldn't just let him get away with his heinous sin. Rory was acting as if we could just move on, patch it up. Could I even consider that idea? Was I going to stand by my man? He had to pay for his actions. He couldn't just get away with it.

Then again, plenty of marriages had survived affairs. Survived, maybe. Forgiven, maybe. Forgotten, impossible.

I saw two paths the rest of our lives could go down. I could instigate a long and painful divorce, which would rip Jasper apart. It would rip me apart. Rory and I would spend a year or two fighting over custody and money, and Jasper would go to college a broken man from a broken family.

Or there was another way. Maybe Rory was right. I would never have told him my revelation at the moment, and it wasn't about him at all. It was about me being selfish and me looking out for my son. What would be best for us? There was the second way of somehow trying to get over Rory's screwup. I could do what other wives of political figures had done. I'd kick him out and make him pay, but eventually, I'd let him back in. Maybe Rory was right. Maybe he was changing. I'd seen more of the old Rory that week than I had in ten years. But, then again, why would he go out and look for another sexual partner? What woman would want to risk ending up in the sequel to his previous sex video?

I said, "I can't talk about this anymore. Not right now."

"I understand. Can I sleep downstairs on the couch or do you want me to leave?"

Through a sudden burst of tears, I said, "I don't know. I don't care. Nothing matters right now. Just get out of my face."

"I will make this right, Margot. I promise you I will make this right. I will seek help. I will accept full responsibility. I'll never talk to Nadine again. She's gone. She knows it. Please, just don't shut me out forever. Let's put this broken road back together."

He'll accept full responsibility? Who else should accept it?

Nadine was gone forever? Only because they had been caught. All words. Just words. Two marriages and families ruined by something that wasn't necessary. Not even love was involved. Why do it? Don't shut *him* out forever? He'd shut me out! My thoughts ran rampant. I turned on the hot water, drowning the noise in my head.

He said he would deal with the press at the end of the driveway. How responsible of him.

I was too exhausted to respond.

10

LOVED ONES

As you might suspect, I didn't sleep well. As in, I didn't sleep. My night consisted of tossing, turning, thinking, and crying. A burning smell from the other room had settled into our bedroom and served as a constant reminder of all the bad that had happened. Throughout the night, I held Philippe like someone was trying to steal him away from me. Though he couldn't understand what I was going through, his interest in my emotional state told me that he understood in a deeper way that something was wrong, and he cared. That's why I loved animals.

Rory wasn't in the house by the time I walked downstairs early in the morning. The doors were locked, and the alarm was on. Usually, I can hear him set the alarm, but I must have been too out of it to hear the annoying robotic voice confirm, "System armed." I disarmed the alarm, let Philippe out into the backyard, and started a pot of water. I stared off into space as I waited for a boil. Every action I took felt slower, like I was moving underwater.

I can't imagine what I looked like. Makeup? Ha! I was too afraid to look in the mirror, but I could imagine the monster I'd see. If I were to leave Vermont today, I could pack all my belongings in the bags under my eyes.

I let Philippe back in, fed him, and made my coffee.

Mug in hand, I walked to the front door and peered out the side windows. Fortunately, there was no one in the driveway. Part of me feared a swarm of reporters would be waiting to snap the first shots of the heartbroken spouse. I entered the living room and turned on the gas; the flame caught with a flash of blue light and a loud puff. I settled into a comfy chair and pulled a blanket over my legs. The lights of the Christmas tree were still on from the night before and twinkled as if the Christmas spirit were still strong in the air. I sipped my strong coffee and waited for the caffeine to give me a fighting chance to handle the day. I'd been dreading this moment, but a part of me felt it had to be done. I had to get online.

I thumbed through my phone first. The first message I saw was a text from Rory. He said he'd be back later and that two off-duty officers were parked at the end of the driveway. No one could pass without my approval. In his message, Rory left me an officer's number. A text from Jasper said he'd be landing at two that afternoon. I waded through the rest of my messages. Apparently, I had people who cared about me. I couldn't respond to them, though. Why would I? I could have lied and typed, *I'm okay! Don't worry about me!* No, I'd reach out to everyone later. The last message had come from Erica five minutes earlier saying she was on her way over. I texted that I'd let an officer know, so she could pass through. I needed my best friend.

I called the number Rory had sent me and told the officer

to let Erica in. I told him Jasper would arrive later. "Please don't let anyone else in without calling me," I said. "I'll have my phone."

I eventually powered on my laptop. Putting off my daily habit of reading the news, I ran through my emails. So many friends and family members had reached out to me. I'm not sure their caring comforted me, but it at least reminded me that I wasn't totally alone. The caring messages also reminded me that so many people close to us were aware of what had happened. Though I knew I would read my news feeds, I wouldn't dare check social media. The idea of Rory's infidelity garnering clicks on Facebook and Instagram terrified me.

Then it was time. I sipped my steaming coffee and dove into my regular news channels. Thank God, it wasn't me front and center. I guess that was nice. No, Rory had all the attention. The more respected news channels didn't show the blurred-out image of Rory and Nadine. Instead, they featured awful head-lines such as *The Mayor Gets His Last Honk* and *Another Politician Caught on Tape*. Each outlet used stock pictures of Rory that his office had released over the years.

When I clicked on the links, I realized even BBC offered a chance for its readers to view the video that had ruined my family. Though I understood how the media thrives on ratings and clicks, I felt so angry with them for not respecting us. All I could think about was Jasper watching the video. It would be almost impossible for him not see his father cheating on me at some point in the next few days. Jasper would see his father committing one of the most intimate acts you can perform with another person, while breaking the most important promise you could ever make. The video was everywhere; people could hardly avoid seeing it.

The knock on the door startled Philippe and me, causing

Philippe to bark as he ran to the door. Once I saw through the side window that it was Erica, I felt desperate for company.

She gave me a giant hug in the foyer, and I burst into tears. "It will be okay," she said, removing her coat and kicking off her wet boots.

Erica and I shared a teary hug, and then I led her into the living room. I sat back in my chair and pulled the blanket back over my legs. She declined a cup of coffee and sat next to Philippe on the floor, running her hands all over him. As he rolled onto his back and welcomed the attention, I could tell Philippe was happy to escape the sadness for a moment.

I looked down at her and asked, "Is the press out there?"

She nodded. "Of course. Everywhere."

I shook my head. "It's not even eight yet, and they're swarming. What kind of world do we live in where people can make money off another's pain? And why are so many people fascinated with the misfortune of others?"

Erica nodded again. "I know. They're vultures." She put her hand on my knee. "You look awful. I mean, like terrible. The worst I've ever seen."

Words only a best friend can get away with. I couldn't help but smile. "I don't want to look in the mirror."

She smiled back. "I wouldn't, if I were you. You look like you're still made up from Halloween. Have you eaten?"

"Eaten? I haven't eaten this year."

"Let me fix you some cereal or something."

"Cereal?" I asked, with a repulsed look on my face. "Don't you know me? What is this, a truck stop? I've never bought cereal in my life."

"Okay, Mrs. Snobby Chef. Can I fix some avocado toast or whatever it is you people eat in the morning?"

"I can't get anything down right now. My stomach's a mess. I would have eaten every pill in this house, but I don't think I could swallow those either."

She stopped petting Philippe and eyed me, discerning if I was joking. I wasn't. "Don't talk like that. Seriously, Margot. We can joke all morning, but I don't want to hear you talking about hurting yourself."

I nodded. Cried more. We talked about stupid things. The Christmas parade. Hallmark movies. After-Christmas sales. We avoided the serious stuff. At least for a while. I told her about the fire upstairs, and we madly laughed at the absurdity of the incident.

When I returned with a second cup of coffee and nestled back into my chair, she asked, "So what now? I'm sure you've been thinking about it."

I sighed and then laughed to myself. "I don't know."

"What do you mean, you don't know? Surely you're not considering a future with Rory." She tilted her head to the left and asked with one raised eyebrow, "Are you?"

I avoided her eyes and drank my coffee.

"As your best friend, I will rip the Band-Aid off here and now. Right now. Rory Simpson is not good for you. What happened yesterday is a signal you need to make a move. The Big Man upstairs is giving you an out." She hit me on the leg. "Don't you dare think of forgiving Rory for this." She added with disgust, "He's the devil."

"It's so easy for you to say, Erica. The ink was barely dry on your divorce papers when you stumbled upon one of the most amazing men in America. That doesn't happen for everyone."

"Oh, so I'm the only woman in the world who will ever find true love?"

"It's not black and white. What if Rory is my true love? We all make mistakes."

Erica shook her head. "This isn't you. Margot Simpson would never forgive her husband for cheating. You deserve so much more. Are you going to stay married to a man you, yourself, call the dream killer?"

"Like I said, it's not black and white."

"Help me understand then," she said. "Because from where I'm sitting, I see you as a damaged woman who has been broken by a first-class jerk husband who doesn't deserve to breathe the same air as you."

"What if I leave Rory and die a lonely death?" I asked. "What if...what if I never meet someone else? I'm not the kind of person who can be alone forever."

"You're not the kind of person who settles. A man is out there waiting for you. Trust me."

"You don't know that," I said, pulling the blanket up farther. "Besides, it's not about me anyway. It's about Jasper. I don't want him growing up without a father. Even if Rory is not himself lately."

"Not himself? He's the same asshole I've always known."

"He used to be different," I said. "He's different around me."

"That's what every abused woman in America says."

"I'm not abused. He made a mistake."

"You might not be physically abused, but you have to know you're emotionally abused. Jasper would be way better off being raised by you alone. The less Rory rubs off on him, the better. And I don't want to hear all this fear about you not finding anyone else. It's about you, too, Margot. You need to be happy. What? Do you want to raise Jasper in a sad home? That boy deserves better than that. A happy broken home is better than what you'd give him if you stayed with Rory. I can't believe you. How could you even consider staying? This 'thing' would always be in your home, like a hovering dark ominous cloud."

I picked up Philippe and hugged him tight. "Your divorce was different. You guys were a disaster. Talk about abusive. You were abusing each other. I've never seen a couple fight so much. Rory and I aren't like that. We never fight. He's just overworked."

Erica raised her voice. "Overworked? The reason you two don't fight is because you're not even living in the same universe. You tell me all the time he doesn't even see you!"

I audibly exhaled and squeezed Philippe tighter.

Erica sighed. "I'm sorry. I know you don't need all this right now. I know you're falling apart. I just...I care about you, honey. Rory is a selfish prick, and he's never deserved you. Don't even think this was an isolated incident. Cheaters always cheat. He's probably been cheating on you for years."

"That's not true."

Erica shook her head. "Don't fool yourself."

"You don't know him like I do."

"Even if yesterday was the first time, it won't be the last. Not if you give him another chance."

Was she right? Had this been going on for a long time? Had I been living my life in ignorant bliss? I couldn't voice my thoughts to Erica. I ran my fingers along Philippe's snout. "What would you have me do, Erica? What would I do with my life? I've dedicated the better part of twenty years to this family and living in this town. Should I just walk away? Grab Jasper and try to start over in a new town somewhere? Leave my best friend? Leave my home?"

"That's exactly what I think you should do, and if you could see clearly and stop feeling sorry for yourself, you'd realize that's what you're supposed to do. Go open that bed-and-breakfast you won't stop talking about! Go start over. Look at you.

You're the catch of a lifetime. Rory is the only one who doesn't see it. He's an effing idiot."

I rolled my eyes.

Erica put her hands behind her on the rug. "I know you need a little tenderness, but I'm not going to let you fall apart. You were there for me during my divorce. You told me I'd find someone better. I said you were crazy. I'll never forget what else you told me that day. You shook your finger and said, 'He's holding you back, Erica. You could be so much more.' I'll never forget those words. Now it's time you take your own words to heart. Take his money, take his son, and get out of here. Go chase your dream."

"Where would we go?"

She raised her voice again. "Anywhere with bed-and-breakfasts. Or someplace where one is needed. Last time I checked, that's every inhabited place on earth."

I took a long breath and said, "My real dream is to raise my beautiful son with my husband. My dream is to be a homemaker and a good wife. My dream is to be the most supportive partner of all time. I don't need to go somewhere else to chase my dreams." I hammered my clinched fist through the air. "My dream is right here. I just have to swallow my pride and forgive him. Why should my whole life be turned upside down? I didn't do anything wrong!"

Erica shook her head again. "You can have all that with a new man—a trustworthy man—and you can have the life Rory never let you have. And, you might not believe it right now, but it's possible that you can have a new life without another man." She wagged her finger at me. "You know what this is? This is you on the dream killer's leash. He's taken your heart and soul. Damn it, Margot. Break free of this man. If you let him talk his way out of this and take him back, will you ever really be able to trust him? You didn't know what was going on before. Will you trust that it won't happen again? And, even if it doesn't, will you believe in your heart of hearts that it's not going on? Every time Rory is out of your sight, will you wonder if he's with someone else? Think about it. You'll always wonder."

I lost patience and said, "I see nothing wrong with at least considering standing by him. He was thinking with his penis. He isn't the first. It was a mistake, and it happens all the time. I can't let the fact that it happened so publicly make it a bigger deal than it is. A strong marriage means standing by your partner no matter what. Fighting through the hard times until you're both sitting in rocking chairs in some nursing home holding hands. That is my dream."

Erica wasn't going to let me off the hook. She drilled me with, "Sticking together doesn't mean accepting deliberate and unwarranted betrayal and possibly leaving the door wide open to a repeat performance." Then, using my own words against me, she repeated what I'd told her during her troubling times, whispering as if resting her case, "He's holding you back. You could be so much more."

I put my hands over my face and rubbed my eyes. I said, "Having a child changes things. It's not about me anymore."

"You couldn't be more wrong, my friend. You couldn't be more wrong. You need to show Jasper how strong you are and how he should live his life. Don't show him how to compromise, show him how to live. You can't believe Jasper would want you to sacrifice your happiness for him. Think about it."

Clenching my fists again, I looked at my best friend and said, "Stop. Please. Just stop."

She raised her hands in the air in surrender.

11

FATHER AND SON

B y the time Erica left, I was lost in confusion. I had hoped she would come to comfort me, but it felt more like she'd arrived with an agenda. I understood her point, though. She was right to speak her mind. I did the same thing to her during the end of her first marriage. Sometimes best friends aren't there to cheer you up, they're there to prop you up.

Still, Erica didn't understand my particular situation, and she didn't understand Rory either. Regrettably, I'd told her over the years all the bad things about Rory, and we'd made fun of him. I'd fueled her opinions of him. But I hadn't told her enough about the good parts of him. Now, I wished I had.

When Jasper finally arrived, as Philippe barked at the door, I tried to wipe the sadness from my eyes. I'd already showered and changed and applied plenty of makeup. Still, there was no amount of makeup that could cover up the pain. The moment I wrapped my arms around my son, I knew we were forming an even stronger bond. No matter what happened going forward, whether we stayed or left, it was now and forever Jasper and Mom against the world.

Jasper stood in the foyer looking at me through his thick-framed glasses. Though he had grown up so much, it was hard for me not to see the young boy who used to beg to visit the playground. He wasn't that boy anymore, though. In only a couple of years, he'd be living on his own. As always, he dressed well and very much looked like a budding musician with his shaggy hair, brown corduroy pants, and green cardigan. He happily embraced the eccentric side of being an artist.

I hugged him again and said, "You know we're going to be all right, don't you? It's just a bump in the road."

"Stop it, Mom." He deflected my protective instincts and turned his love toward me. He looked at me and held my face in his hands. "You don't need to protect me." He looked deep into my eyes. "Tell me. How are you?"

I scrunched my brow in shock. "How am I? How are *you*?"

"I'm fine. I'm more worried about you than anything else."

I nodded. "I'm glad you're home, honey." I refused to cry in front of him and tensed my muscles to suppress the sadness.

We searched each other's eyes for answers.

In the kitchen, while I prepared him a veggie sandwich, we talked about his time in Texas. After putting extra care into his sandwich, I placed the plate in front of him, and he ate hungrily.

In between bites, he asked, "Where is he?" Obviously referring to his dad.

I stood on the other end of the island, resting my hands on the granite. "At his office trying to figure out his next moves. He's coming home soon to talk to you."

Jasper set down his sandwich. "I don't want to see him."

"I know." I nodded. "But the three of us need to talk. I know it's not fair, but with all this press around, we need to meet as a family and figure out what to do. We can't hide in this house forever. We have people who care about us. We all need to talk."

He returned to his sandwich. I sat on the stool next to him. At least we were together.

I asked, "Do your friends know?"

He looked at me, smiled sadly, and took a bite.

I said, "Dumb question, I know."

Halfway covering his mouth, he replied, "There may be people at the North Pole who don't know yet."

I shook my head. "Nah, I doubt it. I can almost hear Santa's elves gossiping about us now. I'm pretty sure everyone knows."

He smiled. "Then the worst is over, I guess."

There we were, connecting. Uniting. Us against the world. Forever bound.

"Did you know about them?" he asked.

"What? Did I know they were having an affair?" To his nod, I answered, "Absolutely not. I don't even know if this was an affair. I haven't talked to him about it yet. Might have been a one-time thing."

He finished chewing and asked, "Are you going to leave him?"

My eyebrows rose to my hairline. "I don't know."

He nodded slowly, and I didn't know if my son approved of my answer.

"What do you want me to do?" I asked.

He turned to me. "I want you to be happy."

"I am happy. I mean, considering. I'm glad I have *you*."

"Mom, you're not happy. You've been a wreck all year. Are you kidding me? I can't believe you guys have made it this long."

"You knew?" I asked. Why did I never give him enough credit?

"I'm a teenager, not a child. I live here too. You can't hide things. You've spent this whole year trying to be someone you're not. I know you're frustrated with him. Who wouldn't be?"

"Why do you say that?"

"He's a workaholic."

I couldn't believe he knew how bad things had been, despite how hard I'd tried to hide it from him. I said, "I tried to protect you." Jasper always understood things few other teenagers did. He always spoke like he was twenty years older than he was. "How are you so much more grown-up than other boys your age?"

"You know how you feel ignored sometimes?" he asked. "Me, too. Not by you. You're an amazing mom. But Dad...he's checked out for sure."

"He's certainly been sacrificing," I admitted.

"Sacrificing our family."

I found Jasper's eyes. "Do you think I should leave him?"

"I can't answer that for you, Mom. I hate him and I'd like to kill him, but no matter what, I will stand by you. It's not about me. I don't have to live with him the rest of my life."

I put my hand on his back. "You're so good to me, honey."

"You're my mom. I'll always stand by you. If you want to leave him, great. If you want to stay, we'll figure it out. I might never speak to him again, but..." He shrugged his shoulders. "I'll respect your decision, and I'll try to get over it. The question is, how can I help you deal?"

At that moment, the side door opened, and we both froze. You live with someone long enough, and you know when it's his energy entering the space. There's no possibility of it being anyone else. Rory walked through the hallway and entered the kitchen. He looked as bad as I did. In fact, all the politician had been exorcised out of him, and he looked like a deflated balloon. Even in his darkest moments the past few years, he could hide his struggles behind that million-dollar smile. Not today. At that moment, his smile couldn't have been more out of reach. His act of betrayal, being caught and exposed, the public shame and embarrassment of it all, had robbed Rory of his easy smile.

How was it possible that I hated what Rory had done—nearly hated him for having done it—but, at the same time, had this sort of empathy for him?

Jasper didn't turn toward him. He stared at the empty plate with only a few bread crumbs left. He shook his head. A big part of me felt tremendous pride. Our son had drawn a line in the sand and taken my side. I had feared he might blame me for driving his father away. Or both of us at the same time. I was afraid he might run away. Kids can do crazy things when they're in pain. Not Jasper. He wasn't a kid, anyway. Not really.

"There are no words," Rory said.

Jasper groaned. Didn't look up. Still sitting next to Jasper, I bounced my eyes back and forth between them. Before Jasper returned home, I thought it might be easy enough to forgive and forget, but I hadn't realized how angry Jasper was. My son was intent on protecting me.

Rory asked, "Can we talk, Jasper?"

Jasper chose silence.

"I'm going to talk," Rory said. "You don't have to say a word. I know I don't deserve for you to listen. I don't even deserve to be here. But I will say my piece. Then I'll get out of your way."

With his hands at his sides, Rory began a long apology I interpreted as heartfelt. My husband was broken. He was sad. After his attempt at some sort of explanation—how he'd been

drowning in work and life—he pleaded, "Don't give up on me."
He instantly broke into a cry and could barely speak for a while.
Ending his plea, he said, "Please don't give up on me, family.
You're all I have. Let me make this right."

I said, "Rory, these are not decisions that can be made right
now."

My husband raised his hand, that familiar gesture I knew so
well. He said, "I know that. I don't expect decisions to be made
right now. You can take as long as you want. I'm not going
anywhere. I just want to know what I can do for you. How can I
help you both get through this?"

Jasper said, "Don't pretend to care now."

"I would never need to pretend. You two are my everything.
Jasper, things become complicated when you grow older. You
can lose your way. I lost mine. We can get through this. We will
look back one day and know that we stuck together. I can find
help. I can leave the office. I can go back to being a lawyer. I will
focus on family, nothing else. Enough of this "climb to the top"
mentality. It's hell to pay, but if we can find any good out of
what's happened, this whole public debacle, it's that I clearly
see how awful I've been. I'll never slip back to that man again.
What do you say, Jasper? Can we at least try to work through
this thing?"

Jasper slid his plate away and pushed away from the island.
He walked up to his dad, stopping a foot from him. Jasper was
much shorter. They locked eyes, and I had no idea what would
happen next. Had Jasper already forgiven him? Maybe he was
young and strong enough that he could move past it.

Jasper finally said to his father, "You're dead to me." With
that, he turned back and approached me. He offered a faint
smile and whispered that he loved me. It was then that his eyes
revealed the enormous pain weighing him down.

I caught myself from falling as all the air escaped my lungs.

"Jasper," I whispered. I opened my arms to him, but he turned away and left the kitchen. I heard the footfalls as he went up the stairs.

I pointed toward the front door in the other room, and I said to my husband, "Go. Go."

As he turned to leave, I fell to my knees, and my chest collapsed.

12

A DREAM COME TRUE

How is it that some people become depressed and stop eating for weeks? It's the perfect diet. Almost worth the depression. I, unfortunately, don't fit into this category.

Two days after the media broke the news, complete with a sexually explicit video showing my husband cheating on me, I broke down. When dealing with emotional turmoil, some might not be able to eat a morsel, but I tossed my diet out the window. After all, I do cook my feelings, and when I'm depressed, I eat them too. All of them, every morsel in sight, like Pac-Woman. Chomp. Chomp. Chomp.

What the heck was the point of eating air anymore?

Though the news of my husband's sexual misconduct wouldn't fully go away for months, our public debacle was no longer the headline-breaking news alert on local news programming, and our story was no longer front-page news in the local newspapers. The lengths of the articles and the sizes of the fonts, thankfully, had decreased and were published a few pages deeper in. But, let's face it, the story would remain in the memories of many for decades. I still hadn't left the house since the news broke. Neither had Jasper. A few news vans were still lingering out on the main road.   .

Rory and I texted each other. Not like we were friends or lovers. Texts about logistics. He'd already done his time with the press, confessing the error of his ways and asking that the media and public respect the family's privacy during this diffi-cult time. Just like that was all there was to it. The four-step program. Indiscretion. Public humiliation. Publicly accept full responsibility. Ask for privacy. Done? Is that supposed to wipe the slate clean? He even stopped by the house several times to talk. We still had lots of details we had to work out if we were ever going to see the other side of this hell.

One by one, I returned calls to my friends and family and thanked them for their concern. I said I'd let them know if I needed anything. Offering to help was what people thought they were supposed to do, but realistically, what *could* anyone else do to help? I didn't even know how to help myself. When people asked, I responded that if they wanted to help, a time machine would be a welcome gift. The person on the other end of the line would generate a nervous laugh, and then I'd promise that Jasper and I would be fine. What real choices did I have? I'd either deal with the tragedy and get by, or I wouldn't. When my friends and family pried and asked if I planned to leave Rory, I wanted to say it was none of their business, but instead, I said I was taking things one day at a time. Why was my decision so important to anyone else who wasn't a member of my immediate household?

My parents offered to stay with Jasper and me for a while. They'd been married for ten years longer than I'd been alive, but I wasn't quite ready for their words of wisdom. I told them

I'd like to see them soon. The truth was that I couldn't imagine them being in Burlington and having to interact with Rory. I knew my parents, and no matter how much they wanted to help alleviate our situation, I knew they were more than disappointed in Rory. They were furious with him. My dad would probably throw a punch, and my mom would probably kick Rory squarely between the legs. No, this was a situation best handled among the people in my immediate three-person family. Well, and maybe Erica.

Besides, I didn't want anyone other than Rory, Jasper, or Erica to see me right now. Erica had been kind enough to go to the grocery store for us, and she'd brought me all my guilty pleasures. When I wasn't cooking, I'd lie in bed with Philippe and watch Hallmark movies, or *Under the Tuscan Sun* for the billionth time, and binge on fries, Cheez-Its, gelato, cookies, and on and on. The behavior was disgusting, and I didn't give a damn! I cooked and ate all day, and though it had only been a few days, I could feel my body swelling back into the heifer size that it used to be.

I cook and eat my emotions, and Jasper plays his. Jasper played and played and played the piano. Occasionally, we'd talk about the future. He'd ask what was next. I'd tell him I didn't know. Because I really didn't. I hoped that answer would soon land in my lap. He'd go back to those ivory keys.

On the fifth day after the video was released showing the dream killer having his ding-dong sucked on camera, as I searched high and low for a way out, I realized what I needed to do. I couldn't believe the decision had taken me this long. Even in the fog of trauma, I should have seen the light.

While I was baking coconut chocolate-chip cookies, Jasper was in the living room singing some sad song, creating the soundtrack for my memories. I found myself thinking about all the kind things I'd done for Rory over the past year, things that should have pleased him, things he should have acknowledged with love. Losing weight. Cutting my hair. Swallowing my pride and allowing him to talk down to me. Taking him meals at work. Loving him unconditionally. It was while thinking about how I let him get away with watching hockey games in bed that the answer came.

There were several nights over the past two months, since the hockey season had started, when I'd found it beyond difficult to concentrate on reading while Rory not only watched his Buffalo Sabres games, but verbally sparred with the commentator, as if the commentator's constant chatter weren't enough of a distraction. Sometimes, I could lose myself in my book—if it was a really, *really* good book—but other times, I'd hopelessly stare at the same page while listening to those two know-it-all men run their mouths full blast. If I were anything less than a Superwife, I would have asked Rory to go downstairs so the bedroom's atmosphere would be more conducive to relaxing and sleeping, but I was focused on pleasing him.

Though I don't care for hockey, I couldn't help but absorb some of the ideas behind the sport. I remembered a match two weeks earlier when the commentator had been going on and on about how good the Sabres looked, but that they would have to stick to their game all season long if they wanted to reach the playoffs. The man went on a long diatribe about how, as the season progressed, so many teams unnecessarily changed their habits, their plays, their plans. He said that even though the matches would become more important, they shouldn't change how they played a winning game. They would have to play the same caliber of hockey that had led them to the playoffs. I recalled how jarring it was for me when Rory shook the bed while throwing his fist into the air and yelling, "Exactly!" as the man finished.

By the time I'd pulled the cookies out of the oven, I was convinced I was on the right track with my own plan. I can already feel you disagreeing with me. I know you're saying something like, "Don't you dare compare your current relationship and situation to the Stanley Cup playoffs."

Well, you know what? That's what I did, like it or not.

You weren't there.

Maybe you're a woman who had a cheating husband, and you left him. Maybe you went on to live a happy life. Good, I'm so happy for you. Let me tell you though, a lot of other women have been in our predicament, forgiven their husbands, and gone on to live amazing lives.

I wasn't ready to say goodbye to Rory or our marriage. Not yet. And I knew what I had to do. I was in the final match of saving our marriage. We had arrived at the Stanley Cup Playoffs. His infidelity was a goal for the other team. That didn't mean I had to give up. Though we had experienced the ultimate setback, he was awakening, and he was seeing me again. For days, I'd seen the real Rory emerging. I enjoyed an IMAX-worthy glimpse of the man I had fallen in love with during our lovely home date the day before the news broke. Since he'd been humiliated on national television, I'd been experiencing even more. He listened like he used to, and he spoke without the politician's fake enthusiasm that had always made me question his motives.

Why should I stop now?

Sure, I could have looked at that night as a redirection of his attraction. Maybe he was falling so hard for Nadine that his sexual urges had reawakened. Maybe he was in a fog of his own —one of lust, and that lust was directed toward me for a minute. Perhaps he would have porked a squirrel that night if the animal had been at the right place at the right time.

I didn't think that was the case, though. I knew the Rory I'd married, and the man who'd slept with me that night was him. He was coming back! I couldn't let this little slipup destroy all the hard work I'd put in. I couldn't let myself be so close to the finish line, only to stop shy.

Like a member of the winning team, I had to continue playing my game. I had to do what kept working. Somehow, I needed to forgive him and move forward. Judge me all you want. I wanted my family back. For better or worse, damn it. For better or worse!

In sticking to the game, I would need to release the Stanley Cup pressure building up inside me. If I could somehow swallow (ugh, what a terrible word, considering his offense) my pride, look past his infidelity, and continue being the perfect wife, then I would have to find a release. And I don't know about you—if you've hung around for the end of this love story —but I didn't think mismatching socks would cut it. Nor would scrubbing the toilet with a toothbrush. Stabbing him with skewers might have worked, but wouldn't violence defeat the purpose? That little skewer daydream, by the way, scared the hell out of me, and I must tell you it wasn't the only violent one I'd had in the past five days. I'll spare you the details, though. Even I have to respect some boundaries. Let's just say that hurting my husband during my soaker-tub daydreams became one glorious way to turn the valve.

Anyway, what pressure release was worthy of a Stanley Cup finish to my year? The answer was on the tip of my tongue.

Considering my decision to stick with the plan, I didn't touch a cookie as they cooled in front of me. Back to the diet, back to air. I put a couple of warm cookies on a plate and took them to Jasper. He was playing Liszt from memory. Though I didn't have his skills or talent, I was no slouch when it came to understanding the emotional and technical aspects of music, and I could tell how well he was playing. You don't win the lead in big productions without being good at what you do. I could list my insecurities, failures, and weaknesses for as long as you want to listen, but the one thing I never doubted was my strength as a musician. I sat and listened to him play—the way he struck the keys, the notes he let linger, the personal stamp he put on the piece.

Something was different.

Tears pricked my eyes as the beauty of his music overwhelmed me. I'd never heard him play so well. Not with such emotion. From my healthier vantage point, if I could point to the best thing that resulted from what Rory had done to our family, it's that Jasper took a giant step as a musician that week. He was no longer a kid running from competition to recital, going for the win. He wasn't playing like a student anymore. There was a growth, a maturity to his playing. Unfortunately, perhaps he was drawing from the angst he'd been forced to endure. Over the past few days, he'd become a professional. Yes, he'd get better and never stop honing his craft, but he had reached a level that very few musicians ever would. It made me sad that I'd been thinking so much about myself, but his playing at that moment was him telling me he'd be okay no matter how things unfolded.

As my son played his heart out, achieving his dream, I thought of my own dreams and almost felt jealous of my son's ability. He hadn't yet graduated from high school, but he had it all figured out. What about me? What about my dreams? I couldn't let Rory steer me away from my destiny. I wondered:

What if I could do it all? What if I could get my family back and have a bed-and-breakfast?

I smiled devilishly. Rory could never refuse me now. Maybe I could turn this devastating week into a good thing; Jasper had. Not wanting to disturb him, I left the cookies on a nearby table. Fully enthused about this idea of having it all, I took my laptop to the kitchen, settled in at the island, and found my favorite real estate website.

Trying not to salivate at the tray of cookies on the stove and that delicious aroma, I entered my criteria and searched for results. I wanted nothing less than five acres. Though I wanted to expand the search outside Burlington, I knew it would be a bad idea. It would only be sad to find the place of my dreams if it weren't close enough. There's no way I could deal with an hour-long drive. Even if someone else ran the place, I felt like I'd hate that drive after a while. The property had to be within thirty miles of Burlington. Knowing I didn't want to endure a massive renovation, I only searched for commercial properties. No way did I want to rip up an old home and add bathrooms.

There were quite a few results, but I'd done enough realty research over the years to eliminate the listings that didn't stand out. I clicked through pictures. Though I hadn't found what I was looking for, I was getting closer. I noticed I was even sitting up a little too straight, a bit too excited. Rory had no idea what he was getting ready to buy.

After thirty minutes of clicking and searching, I chose the three listings I wanted to see. Immediately! Each one had its individual charm. As I clicked through their pictures, I imagined the things I'd do, starting with the area surrounding the inn. Would there be chickens? What do you think? I'd have more chickens than anyone else in Vermont. Would I stop

there? No, no, no. This would be my farm sanctuary. Margot's
Ark. Rory didn't have a "no" left in this marriage.

I stared at one inn for sale called The Sage Wind. The
photos showed a magical backyard with ancient oaks. The
picture had been taken in the fall, and the leaves were changing. I saw exactly where I'd put the chicken coop. I imagined an
idyllic scene with my little hens running around, pecking the
grass. I saw turkeys—happy turkeys we'd save from Thanksgiving dinners. I could see Philippe running around with a pack
of friendly dogs. They were doing their best to herd my sheep. I
even thought about horses. This property was big enough. A
B&B and Margot's Ark would be a lot of work, but I was ready
to start.

I hated, as in, HATED, the kitchen. I'd rip out the heinous
big-box store cabinets, and I'd have to replace all the fixtures.
The inn wasn't exactly move-in ready. I'd have to tear down a
wall or two. Replace some windows. Rip out the track lighting
and add a few sconces. Little things that could be done within a
few months.

The owners were offering to sell the property with the
furniture, but their taste was stuck in the seventies. I'd prefer to
have the total asking price reduced, not to include the furniture.
But if that turned out not to be an option, I imagined a giant
yard sale the moment I closed on this place. Then I'd visit every
antique shop and yard sale within one hundred miles looking
for replacement furniture; it would be so fun!

The bathrooms were cute, though. Most rooms had claw-
foot tubs, which, as you know, I hold dear to my heart. A guest
of a good inn should always be able to enjoy a warm soak after
a long day that resulted in tight muscles, whether from the
stress of a business meeting or from fun activities like biking
and hiking.

My brain swelled with excitement. I thought about the soft towels I'd offer and the organic shampoos and conditioners. My beds would be the comfiest in the state. I had all sorts of ideas on what art I'd hang. We'd have to install a fountain in the backyard. News of my inn would spread, and the results of my eye for detail would draw people from all over New England, who'd want to experience my vision. Before I actually exploded, I needed to see those houses.

I picked up my phone and stared at it, wondering if I should call Erica, because she was a realtor. I could have called the listing agent of each property, but Erica would absolutely kill me. Even if I ended up loving what I found and used Erica to close the deal, she would kill me for not having contacted her immediately, and she'd have every right to.

Telling her my decision regarding Rory, however, seemed like the worst idea on earth. She still didn't know about my pressure-cooker releases.

What to do? What to do? I looked at the freshly-baked coconut chocolate-chip cookies and wanted one so badly.

What to do?

I needed to call Erica. Might as well get it over with.

When she answered, I said, "You will not be happy with me, but I've made some decisions and want your help."

"What are these decisions?"

I wasn't ready for her to go off on me, so I offered her the minimum amount of information. "It's a long story, but it involves buying my bed-and-breakfast."

"What!" she screamed. "You're going to do it! I'm so proud of you."

I smiled. She would be proud until I told her I wasn't leaving Rory. I said, "I'll send you links to the three places I want to see, and if possible, I want to see them today. Can you make that happen?"

"Sure, send them. You're not going to tell me more?"

I hesitated and then, "I'll tell you in the car while we're driving over."

"Wow, you're leaving the house today?" she asked. "Are you ready?"

I looked out the kitchen window toward the forest. Jasper was still playing his little heart out in the living room. I was becoming afraid of everything outside my house, which was a terrible feeling. I answered, "Ready or not, I can't stay in here forever."

"I'm coming to pick you up right now. Send me the listings. I'll set up showings on the way."

I smiled and returned my eyes to the laptop. "I'll send them to you right now."

~

WHILE CROSSING town in her new Mercedes, I told Erica my decision on the drive toward the first place on the list, and I even told her about my retaliation—all the releases I'd been enjoying. I told her about unplugging Rory's phone, mismatching his socks, mixing up his shoes, hiding his slippers, deleting his games; and then I gathered up the nerve to tell her about scrubbing the toilet bowl with Rory's toothbrush. I expected some laughter, but she stayed completely silent as I gave her the details.

After a slight pause, she reluctantly replied, "You're crazy. You know that, right? No one in her right mind does those things."

Her sobering comment lowered my enthusiasm level to a crawl. "It worked."

She started to say something and then held back.

"What?" I asked, eyeing Erica and then the mini hula girl dancing on the dashboard. I felt like both of them were judging me.

"It didn't work, Margot. Your husband cheated on you. I don't see how you think you've gotten him back."

I tried to convince her I knew what I was doing. "Trust me. He's there. I have him right where I want him. He said he'd even resign if I want him to. He will definitely buy me this bed-and-breakfast."

"I hate to rain on your parade, honey, but your buying this place is just a poor attempt at filling the hole in your heart."

I was tired of her trying to convince me to leave him, and my patience was wearing thin. "Look," I said, "I knew you'd kill me if I didn't call you to see these places, but I can't have you trying to persuade me to divorce him every time you open your mouth."

Erica shook her head. "I can't allow my best friend to walk through life with one foot in the grave. I feel like you've given up on yourself. It's like all you care about is Jasper and his future. You wouldn't dare force him to grow up without a father, even though you must realize Rory stepped out of the father scene a long time ago, and you're not even considering yourself in this equation."

"Why are you being so harsh? What's wrong with me wanting Jasper to grow up in a two-parent home?"

"Because Jasper's father is an asshole. He's somehow put a spell on you that makes you think he loves you. Where is he right now? He's probably with that girl."

"No, he's not. He will never see her again."

Erica rolled her eyes. An incoming call saved our conversation and emotions from further escalation. For a minute, at least. Erica answered via the display on the console. It was the listing agent for one of the homes. She would meet us in twenty minutes!

Returning to our dangerous chat, Erica said, "Look, l know you're tired of hearing it from me, but that doesn't mean I will stop. I swear, Margot. You remind me of an anorexic. Everyone around you sees the problems, sees the only clear solution. Everyone but you! That's basically your problem. You still don't think you're skinny enough!"

"Please turn the car around," I said, looking out the passenger-side window. "I can't keep listening to you."

She touched my arm. "I'm sorry, Margot."

I still didn't look at her. "Please don't make me feel any worse than I already do. Looking at houses together is supposed to be fun. You're the one who told me to chase my dreams, and I *will* start my own bed-and-breakfast."

"I'll tell you one more thing, and then I'll shut up if you want me to. You can't chase your dreams with an albatross around your neck. That man is holding you back."

"That man is the father of my son. He's my best friend."

Erica lowered her voice. "I dearly love you, Margot, but we will have to agree to disagree. There's not much more I can say."

I finally turned to her. "You know I appreciate your caring for me, but this is my decision, and I will stand by him. He's paying for his actions. The entire world knows he screwed up. He will deal with that for the rest of his life. I'll never let him live it down. He owes me forever." I was about to rip the mini hula girl off the dashboard and toss her out the window.

"If you only knew how unhealthy you sound right now," Erica said.

I let my head fall back to the headrest. I covered my eyes. Do all the people I know think they know what's best for me? They can't know. Every marriage is different, and no one can know what it's like for me unless she's walked my exact path in my shoes.

While I wallowed in my thoughts, Erica remained silent and kept her eyes on the road. When we saw the first place, I hated it. Possibly because I was so exhausted from our conversation. We couldn't reach the agent for the second inn. It was still occupied, so we did a quick drive-by and got a good look from the car. I didn't love this one either.

I was losing faith, but the third place wasn't so bad. I felt some excitement—not that love-at-first-sight-we-were-meant-to-be-together kind of excitement, but I was open to considering it. Like my own home, the property had a nice long driveway and felt private. There was a pond with a tiny row boat flipped over on the shore. Very cute. Inviting. The property was a little steeper and more rolling than what I'd hoped it would be, but it could work.

The agent was waiting for us. He was a young man with a blond beard, and Erica couldn't help flirting with him as we walked through the house. "I could make this work," I said to them both. Maybe I was a little less than totally enthusiastic, though.

"Yeah," the man said, "it has such nice bones. Have you run a bed-and-breakfast before?"

"Only in my dreams."

"The owners did a great job for a long time, but they're getting older, and she's had some health issues. They're ready to accept an offer."

"It's only been on the market a few weeks."

"Yeah, but they want out. It's time."

As we left, I tried to convince myself that this place could be the one of my dreams. It wasn't perfect, but no place would be perfect. This place had good bones, it was located only a few miles away from our house, and the sellers were eager to move.

I looked at Erica. "I know you think I'm crazy. Unhealthy. Whatever. I want that house. Please call the agent and figure out how low the sellers will go."

Erica was frustrated with me, but knew she couldn't say any more bad things about my husband. "I say we put in an offer $25K less and test the water." She added, "Do you want to talk to Rory?"

"Yeah, but I'll talk to him later. Go ahead and draw up the papers. Rory doesn't have anything to do with this decision. I'm buying this place whether he likes it or not."

Still, I knew I'd have to talk to him. Jasper first, and then Rory. As Erica drove me home, I texted Rory. *It's time to come home.*

Rory wrote back in less than a minute. *Okay.*

I felt my anger dissipating. It'd been only a week since he'd been caught cheating on me, and I'd already bounced back. One thing I knew about myself was that I had to focus on something good to distract me from the bad.

13

ALIEN

My heart pounded as I raced around the house turning on lights. I made sure the Christmas tree was lit and the fire burning. I wanted there to be light in our lives.

Upstairs, I knocked on Jasper's door. "Honey, family meeting downstairs."

He didn't answer and I assumed he was wearing his headphones, listening to music.

I knocked louder. "Jasper!"

He eventually answered the door with one side of his white Audio-Technica headphones pulled away from his ear. "Hi."

"Your dad's coming over," I said. "Can we have a family meeting?"

Jasper nodded. "Give me a minute."

When he joined me in the living room, I said, "I've made some decisions."

"Good, Mom." From his attempt at enthusiasm, I could tell he was trying to be brave. "What kind of decisions?"

"Let's wait for your dad to arrive, okay? He'll be here any second."

Jasper sat at the piano and played a major key run in a high register. His music could always calm me, and I felt my racing heart settle as I drew in a couple of deep breaths and let him take me away. He stepped on the sustain pedal and began stacking notes on top of a major 7th chord. I closed my eyes and let the sounds wash over me. He removed his foot from the pedal, and a stark silence stung the air. I could hear in his heavy breathing the anticipation of Rory's return. Jasper tickled the silence with his right hand as he eased into a soft soothing melody. Once he'd established a theme, he used his left hand to thunder through a powerful chord progression that tugged at my heart.

As Jasper reached a final dramatic crescendo in his beautiful improvisation, the front door opened. He stepped on another pedal and stabbed one last chord, letting it reverberate throughout the house. Throughout my soul.

God, I hoped I'd made the right decision.

Rory removed his jacket and entered the living room. His sweater looked big on him, like he'd lost a lot of weight in the past few days. Much like my own, the bags under his eyes said it all. This had been the worst week of our lives. "Hi, guys," he said, as he went for a chair on the opposite side of the coffee table showing off my linen Christmas runner. I could see that he was nervous. Uncomfortable. Filled with anticipation.

I smiled with everything I had. "Hi."

Jasper spun around on the piano bench to face us both, but he didn't make eye contact with his father.

Jasper didn't see that Rory smiled in his direction. Rory's eyes shifted from Jasper to me. "I've missed you two," he confessed.

I hadn't been so nervous in years. Collecting my thoughts, I placed my hands on my lap and said, "My loves, I've been thinking. The past few days have been horrendous, and I've tried desperately to make sense of what's happening." I looked at my husband. "I've tried desperately to find a way to forgive you. Or at least, to understand." I shook my head. "None of us is perfect, but what you did is so beyond a mistake. It cuts the head off of our love. How can I look past it? How can I ever love you again?"

Rory opened his mouth to speak, but I waved him off and added, "But I want to try. I'm not going to leave you. You don't deserve me, and you don't deserve a second chance, but I'm going to give it to you. Because of the promise I made to you, and because I believe you're a better man than the one who committed this vile act, I am going to allow you back into this family, and I'm going to put everything I have into forgiving you and loving you again."

Rory dropped his head, covered his face, and his shoulders racked as he broke into a sob. I looked over at Jasper, who'd crossed one leg over the other and was hunched over with his head resting in his hand. He was staring at the rug. He wasn't showing any empathy toward his father.

Rory looked up through teary eyes. "I won't mess this up. I swear to God I won't mess this up. I'll give you reasons to love me again." He cast his eyes over to his son. "You, too, Jasp. I'll earn back your respect and love. I swear to you."

Did he believe that? Did he believe he could earn back something that he hadn't valued enough to keep in the first place?

Jasper continued staring at the rug.

"Jasper," I said. He finally broke his stare and looked at me.

"What do you think? Can we do this? Will you support my decision?"

He looked off to the right, but not at his dad. Then he returned his eyes to me and said, "I just want you to be happy, Mom."

I smiled, forcing it with everything I had. "I am, honey. I'm happier every day. Marriage is complicated." I gave a nervous laugh. "Life is complicated. Right now, I'm choosing to stick to the promises I made to your father when we married. In return, he has to agree to seek help." I turned back to Rory. "You have to agree to stop overworking. To go to therapy with me. And I want you to resign your mayoral position immediately." I slapped my leg. "No more public life."

Rory nodded.

I almost brought up the inn, but it wasn't the right time. Not with Jasper here. I continued, "Rory, I'd like you to take some time off and focus on your most important jobs. Being a father and a husband. We have plenty of money. You can afford to take time off. Let's regain what we had as a family. If you have a problem with any of it, you'd better speak up now. This is all part of the deal."

Rory cleared his throat and said, "I'll call a press conference in the morning. Thank you, Margot. Thank you." He clasped his hands together. "I promise I will never betray you again. Neither one of you." He looked at Jasper and reiterated, "I'll fix this, son. I'll earn back your trust, your love. I can't tell you how much I regret not only this week but the past few years. Sometimes you sleep through life. That's what I've been doing. But not anymore."

There it was. The start of something new, I hoped. Sometimes severe trauma can bring about dramatic changes.

No, we didn't step into a group hug; it would take a long

time to reach that point. This was no surface wound that would heal quickly. But no one screamed, and I felt like maybe we left the living room stronger than we had been the day before.

That was a start.

Jasper went back upstairs, and Rory followed me into the kitchen. It was time for an adult talk.

"So much to discuss," he said, taking a seat at the island. "Where do we even begin?"

I shrugged my shoulders, tied an apron around my waist, and opened the refrigerator, wondering what I'd cook for dinner. As I looked from shelf to shelf, I felt my chest burning. Something was still wrong. I didn't feel as great as I'd hoped I would. I wanted to hug Rory and tell him we had a lifetime to talk about things. That we were back to normal. I wanted to tell him we hadn't lost a beat. That's what a good partner would have done.

Instead, I could barely look at him. I wondered how he could even talk—how he had the gall to talk. I felt like he was chattering on, almost as if he'd done something as simple as shattering a glass, not like he'd done something as monumental as shattering a family. I stared blankly at the shelf with the condiments and wondered why I couldn't let go easier. I was so far from letting go. In fact, I wanted to scream and stomp the floor. My emotions were in a turmoil. I wanted to lash out.

Closing the refrigerator, I rounded the island and approached Rory. He turned toward me on the stool, and our eyes met. I don't know what he expected, but he didn't see it coming. I slapped him as hard as I could across the face. The sound of the smack echoed across the kitchen.

Without making a sound he raised his hand to touch the red mark I'd left.

I hit him again. And again. He sat there taking it like he

knew he deserved the punishment. I slapped him six or seven times. As hard as I could. I nearly knocked him off the stool.

Tears fell from his eyes. I wanted to scream at him, but I didn't want Jasper to hear. I whispered, "How could you do that to me? How could you do that to Jasper?"

Still touching his cheek, he shook his head and said, "I don't know." How *could* he explain?

I crossed my arms and asked, "Was it the first time? Tell me the truth. You lie to me ever again, and you're gone."

He wiped his wet cheeks. "No, it wasn't the first time."

Even though I'd asked for it, the painful truth turned my stomach. I closed my eyes and clenched my jaw. Once I could speak, I asked, "How many times? How long?"

"I don't know. A few months."

I thought of how nice Nadine had been to me. "You had sex with Nadine?" I uncrossed my arms. "Why am I asking? Of course, you did."

Rory nodded confirmation. He still held a hand to his face. It had to be stinging, not that I cared.

I pointed a finger at him. "Never again. Don't even think about another woman."

He raised his hand. "I would never. I swear on everything that I am." At that point, everything he was didn't amount to much as far as I was concerned.

Now was the time to drop the bomb. The final act in my play, the last goal in overtime. I said, "I found a bed-and-breakfast I want to buy. You will buy it for me. It's part of the deal."

Rory slowly processed this shocking news. He knew I had him right where I wanted him. He dipped his chin. "Where?"

"On the other side of town. Down Eastern Road." I told him the price.

Rory nodded. "If it's what you want."

There it was! Margot goes in for the win!

I reached across the counter and retrieved a stack of papers that I'd printed out. I said, "I want to make an offer tonight. Erica and I saw the property. She sent these over. We're ready to go."

He took the papers and started eyeing them with a lawyer's scrutiny.

"No," I said, "we're not doing all this. Sign them. Don't read them. This is my thing." I stuck a pen in his face.

Rory looked at me and realized I wasn't joking. He took the pen. I watched as he initialed and signed next to where I'd already made my mark.

Looking up, he asked, "Can we go see it?"

"Tomorrow."

He set the pen down. "Can you tell me more? I'd love to hear about it."

"Do you really care?" I asked.

He nodded. "Yes, I really care."

We were already getting somewhere. Of course, he was about to spend a ton of money and wanted to learn about his investment, but still, he asked like he cared. He did care. I knew he did. He was sincere. I can tell when he's forcing it. A woman can tell when her lover is forcing it.

When I finished cooking dinner, I walked upstairs to invite Jasper down. He answered the door with headphones on again. "Will you sit with us for dinner?"

"No, thanks," he said, his hand on the doorknob. "You guys do your thing."

"Can I bring you a plate?"

He shook his head. "I'm okay, Mom. Seriously. I might get hungry later."

I didn't want our future to be like this. I didn't want Jasper to separate himself from us. I didn't want to lose Jasper. I didn't want him to pull away from me because he wanted to avoid his father. There had to be a way to reconcile this familial unwinding.

I nodded and offered a smile. "Can I tell you a little secret?"

"Yeah."

"We're buying an inn. I'm going to open up a little bed-and-breakfast."

Jasper tried again to be enthusiastic, saying, "That's awesome. Good for you."

I played along. "Thanks. I'll need your help, you know. We're going to put a piano in the main room. Will you play for my guests?"

"Of course." He was saying what he thought I wanted to hear, but I knew he wasn't excited.

I smiled again and touched his cheek. "Hey, we'll be okay. Trust me, we'll be okay."

"I know we will."

"Are you mad I'm not leaving your dad?"

Jasper sighed. "It's not my thing, Mom. It's your choice."

What was I supposed to say? Though Jasper was mature for his age, how could he, as a teenager, truly understand life like an adult does?

Rory and I ate in the dining room. I told him my ideas for the bed-and-breakfast. We could open in the late spring. We talked about our next few months. Suddenly, he would have a lot of free time on his hands. I came around and found some happiness as we talked about the details. He was excited to help. I wanted to believe that all we needed was time and a project, and we'd heal. I could see the three of us driving over to our new inn and getting our hands dirty. We could build the chicken coop together. We could pick out the chickens together.

We could go to the local animal rescue and pick out more furry friends. This bed-and-breakfast could be what we do for the rest of our lives.

"What are you going to call it?" he asked, before taking a bite.

"I've been thinking about that. I don't know." I was usually so good at coming up with names, and you'd think I would have been sitting on a name for a long time, this being my dream and all. But I guess naming it would have made a letdown that much more disappointing.

After cleaning up, we both said goodnight to Jasper and climbed into bed. Unsurprisingly, the energy between my husband and me was awkward. Rory was beaten down. He'd been getting hit from all angles. I realized that I couldn't keep hitting him physically, verbally, or emotionally. If I were to forgive him, I needed to do it now. He lay there staring at the ceiling.

I turned toward him and put my hand on his chest. "We will make it." I patted him and said the words that needed to be said. "I forgive you. And I love you."

He looked at me and turned up the corners of his mouth. "I love you more today than ever before. Thank you for believing in me."

Once he was snoring, I lay back on my pillow. For the next few hours, I drowned in my own thoughts. Not about the bed-and-breakfast. Not about good things. All I could think of, all I wondered was...

Why wasn't I happy? Why didn't this feel right? Did I really believe in Rory? Did I really forgive him? Did I still love him like I should? Would we ever get through this? I felt like I didn't even belong in that bed.

I felt like an alien in my own body.

14

ÉPIPHANIE

I woke with the emptiest feeling I'd ever known. I reached over to his side of the bed; Rory wasn't there. I scanned the bedroom through foggy eyes. Philippe was on the rug, sleeping on his back with his legs in the air.

Feeling like I hadn't slept at all, I closed my eyes and tried to drift away, but the emptiness wouldn't let me. It wasn't that my mind was racing. More like I'd been stepped on and kicked so badly that even sleep was a chore. I forced myself out of bed and stumbled like a zombie down the stairs. I crept past Rory sitting in the living room and went into the kitchen, where I found the coffee still warm in the carafe.

I sat at the island, slouched over, with what had to have been a dumb look on my face. As I gulped the coffee like a ship-wrecked woman who'd found a bottle of fresh water, I waded through the sea of my thoughts. What was wrong? I'd gotten Rory back. Jasper was home. We were safe. The outside world would be cruel to us for a long time, but we were together. How could I possibly feel so deflated?

Rory entered and kissed the back of my head. "Good morning, dear."

I intended to say, "Good morning," but my words escaped as a grunt, instead. I must have been experiencing some sort of a delayed reaction to what had gone on over the past week, because his kiss and his voice spread through me like a virus, and an immediate rage like I'd never known before rose to the surface. My muscles tensed, and I nearly spun around and swatted him. I stopped myself. Was it always going to be like this? My swallowing my emotions? My trying not to rock the boat?

I breathed through the feeling quickly. Sipped more coffee and took a deliberate breath. As he walked around the island toward the sink, we met eyes for a moment. Tapping into my years on stage, I smiled with everything I had and said, "Did you sleep well? I didn't hear you get out of bed." I didn't want him to see the emptiness, the doubt, the fear, and my newfound emerging rage.

"Very well, thanks. I'd missed being in our bed next to you. How about you?"

"It's really great having you back," I lied.

Rory walked up to the sink and began to refill our water pitcher. With his back turned to me, I glared at the man I'd chosen to forgive. Almost as a non sequitur, I found it repulsive that I'd ever thought he was cute in his pinstriped pajama pants.

Over the sound of the running water, he turned and asked, "Any news about the offer?"

I shook my head. Forcing my words, I said, "No. I told Erica to set up an appointment for us though. This afternoon, after your press conference."

"Great." He turned off the water and acted like this was all normal. "We'll have some celebrating to do."

Celebrating was the furthest concept from my mind. Was he for real? I lied, though. "Yes, we will. Are you sad?"

"To resign?" he asked, putting his hand on the counter facing me. "No. I'm ready. I'm so worn out and broken up over this whole thing, I'm just ready to get out. I'm ready to start living again."

His words sounded good, but they didn't fill my heart. Not like they might have yesterday. Was he broken up over this whole thing? He'd put himself in this position. I imagined it would be quite different if he hadn't been caught. He'd still be carrying on, business as usual. How could he even make this about him being the one who was broken? Unbelievable. I had to leave the room. I couldn't even look him in the eyes.

I mumbled, "Be right back," and left the kitchen in a scurry. I walked into the bathroom and looked at myself in the mirror. Oh, God, the bags. Erica had said I reminded her of an anorexic. I saw my skinniness in a disgusting way. I looked like a skeleton. Saggy flesh draped over sad bones. I looked into my eyes, like really into them. There was no brightness, no life. I looked gray. I felt gray. I felt like a shadow of myself.

Was this more pressure I had to release? It didn't feel like it. More like the opposite. Rather than exploding inside, I was caving in on myself. Imploding.

What was wrong with me?

Returning to the kitchen, I said, "I'm going to climb back into bed." Would staying in bed be my future life? Would it be my way to hide?

Rory was scarfing down some yogurt. As if we weren't living in a continuing nightmare, he replied, "Okay. I need to head to the office and tell everyone. I'll let you know what time the press conference is. Assuming you want to see it?"

"I'm not sure I do," I admitted. "I feel a little sick all of a sudden. Come home afterward. We'll celebrate, okay?" Celebrate? How could I even say that word? Swallowing my disgust, I went up and kissed him on the cheek. "Good luck, dear. I'm happy for us."

A giant lie. Happiness was light years away.

Upstairs, I snuggled with Philippe in the bed. I was too tired to think, but still too tired to sleep. The hollowness consumed me. Tears dripped from my eyes, but I wasn't crying. It felt more like I was drying up, dehydrating. It soon occurred to me that I might be dying. I could see how people can feel so depressed that their bodies follow suit and fail them. My body was becoming more frail, and I thought I could almost feel my bones shrinking.

Lying there, I felt like I was trapped in a coffin, and I couldn't handle it anymore. I jumped out of bed, desperate to escape myself. Have you ever felt that way? Where you couldn't even stand to be in your own skin? You couldn't stand to be *you*. It's the worst feeling, because if there's anything you can't ever do, it's separate from yourself. Not without inflicting harm.

Usually, I can cook my way out of the worst of moods. But, at that point, the thought of cooking made me want to throw up. I never wanted to cook again. I wanted to burn my kitchen down!

What to do?

I looked in the closet at my running shoes. Thought about going for a jog. And then I remembered that there might be lingering journalists waiting to snap a shot of the mayor's wife crumbling amidst the chaos. Especially with the press conference today. Rory's announcement would bring another week of the press camping out in our neighborhood.

Finally, I figured out what to do to keep myself busy. As you can imagine, the house was a wreck. I hadn't let the house-keeper clean this week, because I didn't want anyone in my house, and I hadn't cleaned. Rory had taken out the burnt rug and cleaned the floor of the room upstairs, but the entire upstairs still smelled of smoke. Jasper had tried to help, but I'd always done most of the cleaning, so he wasn't very good at it. Maybe cleaning the house would be a step toward internally cleansing myself.

I feverishly moved throughout the house, working on table surfaces first. Sweat quickly gathered on my brow. Then I cleaned the windows. I scrubbed the showers, baths, sinks, and toilets. Nope, not with his toothbrush. I vacuumed and polished the hardwoods. I started the laundry. Lastly, I entered the kitchen to finish there. I felt horrible in this place that used to bring me comfort, and that feeling scared me. The kitchen was my safe place, or at least it used to be. I put my head down and cleaned. I pulled out all the items from the fridge and scrubbed the shelves. I threw out the old food, as if this simple act might help me throw out all my old emotions.

When the trashcan was full, I removed the bag and navigated our icy back stoop toward the large trash bin. The chilly air felt more cleansing than anything else I'd done that day. I barely looked at the snow on the ground, covering our beautiful yard, as I dropped the bag into the bin. Returning to the house, I almost slipped on the steps on the way back but caught myself on the railing. I put a hand to my heart, thinking of how badly a fall could have hurt. I needed to be more careful.

Back inside the kitchen, I retrieved the small blue recycling bin that was spilling over with the glass jars I'd removed from the refrigerator. I stepped back outside and navigated those slippery steps again. A cold wind rose out of nowhere, and it made me shiver. That's all it took to knock me off balance.

My feet flew forward on the ice, and I fell backward. My lower back hit the edge of a step and my head snapped back, smacking the brick. I yelled in pain. The recycling bin emptied on top of me, and bottles and jars rolled over me and crashed onto the steps, many of them breaking.

I sat up, reached to the back of my head, and felt warm blood trickling from a gash. I examined my fingers as the crimson ran toward my palm. Something kept me sitting there for a few minutes. The pain and the cold woke me like I'd jumped into Lake Champlain, and I actually felt great. In what a spectator might have called a complete lapse of sanity, I broke into laughter, an uncontrollable belly laugh. Blood on my head and hands and savage laughter in my heart.

Then, as quickly as it had come, I stopped laughing and a sense of clarity washed over me. What was I doing? Not on the steps. I mean, what was I doing with my life? Why had I chosen to stay with Rory? Was it because of the promise I'd made in our wedding vows? Was it for Jasper? Was it for me?

Or was it strictly based on fear?

I shook the questions off and carefully stood. It was only natural to be freaking out. Our whole world was changing. Rory was about to dash water on his aspirations and end his entire political career—everything he'd ever hoped for—in order to make things right for our family. I was correct in giving him another chance. We all make mistakes.

I began collecting the empty cans, bottles, and broken glass, dropping them into the blue bin in my hand. Moving too quickly, I reached down for a broken wine bottle and it sliced through my skin. I dropped the glass and cried out as more blood stained my hand.

"What is wrong with me!" I wailed, clutching my arm in pain. "Damn it!"

I looked down at the piece that cut me. The label was still intact. Three words stood out. *Red Mountain Merlot.* In smaller text, *Washington State.* It was the bottle Nadine had given to me, as an act of kindness on the night I hosted our latest event, the bottle of wine I'd grabbed on the way to soak in the tub on the day I saw the video. Something was strange, though. In what I can only describe as an epiphany, the label began to glow with golden light. At least my mind created such an illusion.

A peace washed over me amidst the cold and pain. All my cares drifted off to nowhere.

Why was this bottle glowing before me? Had Nadine been sent by some higher power to guide me? To tell me what I needed to do? Or had the man who'd sold her that bottle of wine played a role in my destiny?

I suddenly saw the truth and for that moment caught a glimpse of the essence of life. I saw everything laid out before me. I saw the complete absurdity of who I had been that year. The not eating, the playing of childish pressure-release games, the faking happiness. Denying the real situation.

The bottle was speaking to me, showing me what to do, where to go.

I could not stay with Rory. I couldn't stay here.

The road ahead would be scary, but I dared not tread down the path of fear, or I might get lost thinking of all the things I'd have to do in the next few months. But that label answered the most difficult question. I didn't know what Red Mountain was. I knew nothing other than what Nadine had told me. An up-and-coming wine region with some of the best wines in the country.

What better place to open a bed-and-breakfast!

There it was. My whole freaking destiny laid out as the result of a slip on the ice and a slice on the hand. I picked up the broken piece and looked harder at the label. I'd been misled by so many false ideas and answers, but this one was different. This bottle had come from the source.

Tossing the piece into the bin, I cracked a grin and, very carefully this time, walked up the steps and returned to the kitchen. Philippe was wagging his tail. I knelt down and laughed with glee as he licked my face. "Big things are coming, my love." I pressed my face against his. "Will you move with me? A big adventure lies ahead."

I stood back up, desperate to do some research. Was I really going to do this! Though I had a valid fear of the unknown, it was the excitement and confidence that fed my soul. Jasper was up and playing piano. I felt the resurgence of life coursing through me as I bandaged my hand and went for my laptop. I sat at the kitchen island and keyed in: *Red Mountain, Washington State.*

I clicked on the images. Sight unseen, this place would be our new home. When the images loaded, I was at once surprised and mesmerized. I'd never seen such a landscape. I'd expected to see lush forest. Some sort of wet climate. Like what you'd expect from Seattle. Red Mountain wasn't that way at all. It was dry, almost desertlike, with beautiful, rolling hills. There were vineyards everywhere! It reminded me of the Tuscany I'd seen in my favorite movie. My eyes bulged as I thought of chasing a dream not dissimilar from Frances's in *Under the Tuscan Sun.*

I saw images of wineries at harvest. I saw pictures of the leaves changing. I couldn't believe I'd never heard of this place. I wondered what it would be like to live there. Was I actually crazy enough to go find out?

Chill bumps rose on my arms. I realized I wasn't being crazy. This moment was the sanest, most lucid I'd been in years. Was this how major life events happened?

Then my heart sank and my smile dissipated. Doubt crept in. What about Jasper? I couldn't take him from his piano teacher, and I most certainly wasn't going to leave him with the dream killer. Whether Rory would change was yet to be decided. No, wherever I went, Jasper was coming with me, but he needed excellent musical coaching. My fingers flew over the keyboard as I searched Washington State for music teachers.

Was this really meant to be or just another fantasy?

The shocking results confirmed that I'd somehow tapped into my destiny. And Jasper's too. According to an article I found in the *Seattle Times*, one of the finest piano teachers on the West Coast had left Seattle to open up a school in Richland, Washington. Richland was fifteen minutes from Red Mountain! My heart raced as I felt the snowball of my destiny barrel down the hill, collecting speed and mass. I felt myself breaking free of the chains. Was I going to do this? A resounding *hell, yes* rose from deep down.

I searched for the lodging options on Red Mountain. It's important to know the competition. Other than a few VRBOs and Airbnbs, there was nothing! No place to stay in wine country. I found a real estate website and searched. Red Mountain was so small I didn't need to filter. There were no commercial buildings available, but there was a house.

Not just any house. There was my home, staring back at me. I clicked on the pictures. It was a Spanish-style house with white-stuccoed walls and a terra-cotta red-tile roof. The inside was to die for, almost exactly how I might have decorated it. The kitchen featured high-end, brand-new appliances, and I could see myself standing on that tile floor, trying out a new recipe.

I read the description below. The house stood on a large piece of land. I did a quick search of zoning laws, and it appeared that I could indeed build my bed-and-breakfast on the same property! What could be more perfect than living a stone's throw away from the inn? As a bonus, there was another piece of property for sale right next to it. Maybe I could buy that too, though the land was much more expensive than the property that I'd been looking at in Vermont. With more online research, I quickly learned that vineyard land of that quality draws a high price tag.

I couldn't wait another moment to tell my son and yelled, "Jasper!"

The music stopped and he came running. "What's wrong?"

"Nothing's wrong, sweetie. Not a thing in the world."

"Oh, my God," he said, looking at me. "What's all that blood?" He pointed to the back of my neck. I'd totally forgotten about having hit my head. As he pointed it out though, I felt the pain rise.

"No big deal," I said. "I fell outside. It doesn't matter. I have huge news."

He pointed at my hand and arm. "Mom, you have blood all over you."

"It doesn't matter." I grabbed his wrist with my bandaged hand. "How would you feel about moving to Washington State?"

"Mom, you need to go to the hospital."

"I'm okay. Seriously. I'm the best I've ever been." I let go of his wrist. "And I'm asking you for real. Do you want to move to Washington?"

"It's too wet there," he said, still shocked over my injuries.

"I'm talking about eastern Washington. The dry part of the state. I found a beautiful house on a gorgeous piece of property where I could build my bed-and-breakfast. And there's a great piano teacher nearby."

"You're serious?"

"Look at me. Does anything about me right now make it look like I'm joking? Let's get out of here."

He smiled. "Why not? Maybe the news of the Simpson family breakdown hasn't made it that far." He dropped his smile and looked at me with concern in his eyes. "What about him?"

I noticed he didn't say *Dad*. I said, "I'm going to leave your dad, honey. I know I've been so wishy-washy, but I made a mistake last night. I can't stay with him. I'm so sorry."

He put his arm on my shoulder. "You being for real? You haven't just hit your head and gone wonky, have you?"

"I've never been more for real."

Jasper nodded. "I'm proud of you, Mom."

"For what?"

"For finding courage."

I pinched my chin as chill bumps rose on my arms. "I lost it there for a minute, didn't I?"

"A minute or two. Now, seriously, let me look at your head."

"Oh, it's just a little thing."

He pulled my hair apart searching for the gash. "You might need stitches, Mom. It's not good."

"I'll have it checked out."

The back door opened and closed. Jasper and I looked at each other, and he took a seat next to me. It was time.

Rory found us in the kitchen and announced, "You are now looking at the ex-mayor of Burlington, Vermont."

"Congratulations," I muttered, wondering how I would break the next piece of news.

"Oh, God!" Rory exclaimed. "What happened to you?" My husband rushed toward me.

I put up my hand to stop him. "I'm fine. I fell outside. It's okay."

He reached out to touch my arm, but I pushed him away. "Stop, Rory. Just... stop."

"What's going on?" he asked, tilting his head.

I grabbed Jasper's hand and found the courage I needed. "We're leaving Vermont. We're moving to Washington State."

"We are?" Rory asked, still looking at all the blood.

"Not you," I replied, maybe a little too harshly.

Rory was obviously blindsided. I knew the look. I'd been there before.

"I'm sorry," I said, "but Jasper, Philippe, and I are going without you." I stood and walked toward my husband. "Rory, I want a divorce."

Wrinkles matted his forehead. "But...what about last night? About what you said?"

"I was wrong. I was trying. I don't want to continue "trying." I wish nothing but the best for you. I know Jasper does too. But you and I can't be together anymore. It was over long before this week. I've just been holding on for dear life. I don't want to have to hold on for dear life anymore. I have to move on. Jasper and I need to get out of here."

Rory dropped his head. "Please, Margot. Let's talk it out."

"Rory, I'm sorry. This is not a topic up for debate."

Rory stood in silence for what seemed like forever. He finally said, "Let's talk again in a few days. We can't rush to conclusions." He scratched his head and left the kitchen. I could hear him break into a sob as he crossed into the living room.

Jasper approached and hugged me. I squeezed my son with everything I had. Sometimes, having each other is all you need. Our bond strengthened as I cried into his shoulder.

"We will be all right," he whispered.

"Yes, we will, my dear. We have a long road ahead, but it will definitely be all right. We're moving to Washington State."

"Shouldn't we visit first? What if it sucks?"

"Do you trust me, honey?"

"Of course."

"We don't need to visit. I'm putting an offer on a house today. As soon as the deal's made, I'll hire movers to transport everything, and we'll drive out there with Philippe and a couple of bags."

He couldn't believe my words. "Right on, Mom. Right on."

Erica phoned as I mopped away my tears. I told Jasper we'd talk more in a little while and then took the call upstairs. Rory was hiding in his office with the door closed.

Erica said, "I see your husband just quit."

"Word travels fast," I said, sitting back on my bed. Philippe jumped up to join me. "In other news, I just told Rory I'm getting a divorce."

Silence.

"Did you hear me?"

Silence.

Louder, I said, "I told Rory I want a divorce. Do you hear me?"

"I hear you," she said. "I'm just...I'm crying."

I smiled. How nice to have a friend who cares so much for you. "You were right all along."

"Uh, yes, of course I was! You finally see the light. My Margot is back."

"I *am* the light," I said.

"Yes, you are."

I ran my hand along Philippe's back. "I have more news. Jasper and I are moving to Washington State." I told her briefly about my morning. Then, "Oh, I guess you need to rescind our offer on the place near here. Sorry about that."

"Guess what," Erica said. "I didn't submit it."

My eyes widened. "You bitch."

"I know."

"You're a terrible real estate agent."

She ignored me and said, "So a bed-and-breakfast in Washington State?"

"In the middle of wine country."

"I'm so coming to visit!" Erica exclaimed.

"I'll have a room waiting. Thanks for being my best friend, Erica. Don't ever let me forget how good you are to me and how much you mean to me."

We both choked up and said at the same time, "I'm going to miss you." We laughed at the timing and said two more words simultaneously, "Me, too."

As I wiped my tears, Erica asked, "What are you going to call your new place?"

I looked up in the air for an answer, and it was waiting for me. "Épiphanie. The French spelling with an accent over the E. To always remember this day. To remember what it's like to wake up from a nightmare and realize you still have plenty of life left to live."

Erica said triumphantly, "You do! You have so much more life to live, and I couldn't love you any more than I do. I'm so proud of you."

Though I knew I'd spend a long time healing, that day was the day I first tasted the greatness of surrendering to life. It's the first day I connected with my elusive higher consciousness. It had taken me this entire year of trying to make my husband see me to realize that what needed to happen was that I needed to see myself.

EPILOGUE
FAMILY FORWARD

You're probably hoping that I'd torn Rory apart as I set my terms in the divorce. That I'd taken all his money. All the furniture. His dignity. Sorry to disappoint you, but I did my best to be civil. We hadn't completed the divorce yet. We had to live separately for six months before we could sit for our final hearing. We were close, but not quite there. We'd done everything else though.

Rory would stay in Burlington and start up his law practice again. He'd found an apartment downtown. We sold the house. It was too big for him anyway. As far as the divorce terms were concerned, I won full custody of Jasper, and I took half of Rory's, well, *our* money. I could have taken more, but I didn't want to start my new life from a place of greed.

The day I told Rory I wanted a divorce, I put in an offer on the house I loved on Red Mountain. Sight unseen. I paid too much, but I didn't want others to see the listing and jump into a bidding war with me. I didn't mind paying the full asking price. According to the realtor I'd found, property on Red Mountain was going up quickly, so it was a seller's market. Not buying that house would have been spitting in the face of destiny. I didn't buy the adjacent piece of property like I'd wanted. I needed to build the inn first and see how much money would be left over. Everyone warned me that building something always cost twice as much and took twice as long as projected. I hoped that wouldn't be the case. This realtor I'd found had already recommended a contractor she really liked and trusted. Hopefully, he would take care of me. Either way, I knew that if it was meant to be, I'd eventually buy the other piece of property.

On a beautiful spring day in Burlington, Jasper, Philippe, and I climbed into the car to drive west. We still hadn't seen our new house on Red Mountain, but it already felt like our forever home. The best part of that day was to see Jasper every bit as excited as I was. We were leaving all the pain and sadness behind.

The movers had left the day before and would arrive before we would. Jasper and I had planned to take our time driving. We wanted to see Little Big Horn, Mount Rushmore, the Badlands, the largest ball of twine on earth—and all the other required stops on a road trip west.

We were traveling light, only two suitcases, a cooler, and a bag of snacks in the back. I'd set up the middle seats with layers of blankets for Philippe, and I'd spent a fortune buying him toys, baked goods, and vegetarian bones.

I started the car, shifted into reverse, and looked at my son. "We've had some good times in Burlington."

He put his hand on top of mine. "I'm ready for better times."

I smiled. "Today is one of the most exciting days of my life, Jasper. I couldn't be more thrilled about the journey ahead."

He held up crossed fingers. "Red Mountain better be cool. I'm trusting you."

"I'm trusting me too. If it doesn't work out, we'll keep going. Nothing will stop us now."

"You're a cool mom. I'll miss my friends, but I wouldn't miss this for the world."

Soon we were on the highway driving west. Chasing a dream. I hadn't lost touch with my husband; I'd lost touch with myself. It was I who needed to wake up. I pushed down the gas pedal, and we rode toward our destiny. I knew we'd be okay.

As we drove over Lake Champlain and crossed into New York, Jasper reached under his seat and pulled out a child-sized keyboard. He hammered out a beautiful version of "Somewhere Over the Rainbow," and I joined him for the chorus.

I sang with him all the way to Red Mountain. Mother and son.

A song and a dream.

Follow Margot and Jasper to Washington State in my novel *Red Mountain*, available where books are sold.

For more books, free stories, updates, and my newsletter sign-up, visit boowalker.com.

boowalker

Please enjoy the following excerpt from *Red Mountain*.

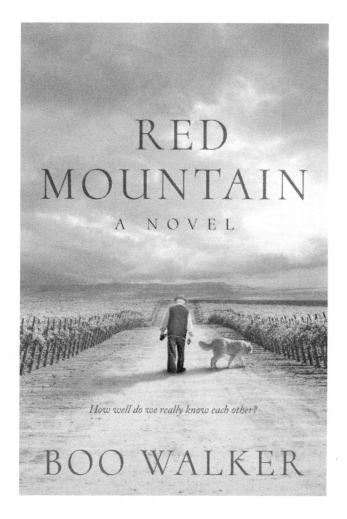

RED MOUNTAIN

Boo Walker

A COYOTE WITHOUT A PACK

Late September, Washington State

Under the light of a wide-eyed moon, Otis Pennington Till strolled into his syrah vineyard, puffing on an unlit briarwood pipe. At sixty-four, and despite a lower back still tender from lifting a wine barrel earlier in the year, he moved with a fair amount of grace.

Not too far away, the coyotes called up into the moonlit big sky night, their howls and yelps disturbing the calm of Red Mountain. He could hear the uneasy *baas* of his flock of Southdown sheep stirring in the pasture below, and he knew his huge Great Pyrenees, Jonathan, was on high alert.

"*Baa* back to you, friends!" he shouted with a faint British accent, the leftovers of his London childhood.

Kicking aside a tumbleweed with his work boot, Otis plucked a few grapes from one of the ten-year-old syrah vines and put them in his mouth. He closed his eyes, and as the skins burst between his teeth, the juice coated his tongue. He hoped to be overwhelmed by the complexity of the fruit, the mouth-watering acidity, the velvety tannins, the elegance. But the nuances he'd grown used to tasting in ripening Red Mountain grapes didn't treat him tonight.

For a couple of weeks now, Otis had been struggling with his sense of smell and taste. When he first noticed the symptoms, he chalked it up to a cold or a hiccup of growing old; perhaps a result of too many hours spent with his tobacco pipe as of late. But his condition was getting so bad that he might be incapable of making wine this year.

Otis spat the seeds to the ground like he was spitting in his opponent's face. He cast his pipe into the dust, cursing.

Trying to wrangle his anger, he filled his lungs with the cool, clean air and gazed at the harvest moon, the bright orange eye of the night. "Please don't take my wine away from me," he begged. "It's all I have. You might as well kill me now."

Otis tossed his tweed cap to the ground. He removed his cardigan and plaid button-down shirt, his boots and trousers and the rest. Naked, he stood tall and proud. Chill bumps rose on his arms. He lifted his hands in the air, as if ready to catch a star. He drew his right hand to his face, kissed his palm, and blew that kiss up towards the heavens, up towards the rest of his family—his sons and wife. "I could be joining you sooner than later, my loves."

Lowering to his hands and knees, he looked back to the moon and howled. Without a trace of self-consciousness, like a child, he howled. As loud as his body would let him, he imitated the wild dogs out there, pacing in the darkness, calling out, singing their songs.

Ahhhhhh-ooooooooooo! Ahhhhhh-ooooooooooo!

Stopping to catch his breath, Otis noticed the coyotes had raised the volume of their own song, perhaps welcoming him.

He could hear the higher pitch of the young ones and the deeper haunting sound of the eldest, and Otis howled even louder and with more heart.

Ahhhhhh-oooooooooo! Ahhhhhh-oooooooooo!

Feeling better, Otis dressed and made way back toward the house at the western end of his forty acres. He took pride in the fact that every square foot of his property was tidy. Despite the occasional strong winds that often brought trash from the road, not even a bottle cap could be found on his land. Every hose was coiled to Army standards. Weeds were virtually non-existent. You could have slept in the sheep corral or dined in the chicken coop. All his energy, all the usual precision of a Virgo that was normally channeled toward the loving and caring of other humans, Otis redirected toward his animals, his property, and his wine.

He entered the stone home he and his wife had built and made way to the study. Most evenings, when he felt too lethargic to tackle anything constructive, he found at least a modicum of solace in gazing at the wall-to-wall shelves lined with his collection of books, all well-read, thoroughly enjoyed, and dog-eared, especially those written by English authors, like Shakespeare, George Orwell, D.H. Lawrence, Graham Greene, and Churchill. He felt a kinship with them, even though he'd been an American citizen since his early teens.

At the touch of a button, Art Tatum crooned from the CD player. Otis poured himself a peaty twelve-year-old scotch from a crystal decanter and carried the glass over to his recliner. Since his wife had died five years before, he hadn't slept in their bed. He couldn't even bring himself to lie down in it. He couldn't bear to revisit their intimate moments there—their naked bodies wrapped around one another, Rebecca stroking his hair and murmuring in her soft morning voice that he missed so dearly, their silly pillow fights and their once-a-month lazy Saturday mornings when they wouldn't get out of bed until noon. Since she passed, he had slept on the couch or in this recliner, a beast of a chair he'd worn in so well that the outline of his body was visible in the cracked, worn leather.

Using a letter opener that had belonged to his father, a journalist who wrote for the *London Telegraph* and the *Bozeman Daily Chronicle*, Otis rifled through the stack of mail. Eventually he drew out a letter addressed in large, flowery handwriting. He recognized it as being from his maternal aunt, Morgan. She didn't believe in computers, she loved to brag, so her correspondence was by virtue of the United States Postal Service.

Just seeing her name on the return address made Otis moan. Morgan was the Queen Bee of Montana—the belle of the ball, but Otis could handle her only in small doses. Her personality matched her handwriting—too big and forceful for her petite body. She'd outlive him by thirty years; he was sure of it.

As always, the letter began innocuously. But Otis was wise enough to expect a surprise. He found it, and the words made him jump to refill his glass. He could hear her high-pitched voice as he re-read the end:

I'm coming to see you, sweetie pie. What's it been? Five years? Since the funerals? Not acceptable. Seems like you and I are the only two of our blood who are managing to survive this sometimes awful world. We should share secrets. I'll be there on Monday. According to the lovely lady at the post office, you should get this letter on Saturday. I didn't want to give you the time to stop me. Make sure you pick up some Folgers and half and half. You know I can't stand that Seattle single-origin crap.

See you very soon,
Morgan

Otis reached for a half-eaten bag of pork rinds and worked his way through them while pondering her intentions. He raised his eyes to the urn that held the last of his wife's earthly remains, the turquoise vessel a gift from a potter friend in Sonoma.

"You wouldn't believe who's coming to town, Bec," he said, setting down his snack. "Aunt Morgan. She's still trying to pair me up with some other girl." He shook his head. "Morgan loved you so much. I don't know why she'd ever want me to replace you."

No one knew Otis had kept his wife's ashes. He'd told her brother and her best friend that he had spread her remains in their vineyard on Red Mountain, as she'd wished. But he liked having her in their home, and he wasn't ready to say goodbye. He stared at the urn for a while, revisiting old memories— trying to focus on the happier ones. Then he bid his dead wife goodnight and returned to thoughts of his impending visitor.

Aunt Morgan. Coming to Red Mountain. What a disaster. She'd been hinting at this trip for months now. She'd decided he was lonely and sad, and it was time he started dating again. She made him feel like he was fifteen with her overprotective smothering. And now she was coming to town.

Involuntarily, Otis's imagination played a series of disas- trous scenarios resulting from her visit; all of them centered on his being embarrassed in front of his friends and fellow Red Mountain inhabitants. Otis knew his reputation on the moun- tain. He was a respected leader, a pioneer, the wisdom bearer, the godfather, the man the young winemakers and grape growers came to see. How easily Morgan could burst this persona, leaving him vulnerable and exposed, to be picked apart and laughed at by the vultures of youth. His thoughts finally faded to black.

He woke in the chair hours later. The window faced the top of Red Mountain, which was about 1,400 feet at its highest point. The sun hadn't quite peaked over the mountain but had brightened the night to a tarnished silver, illuminating the silhouettes of the vines running along the hills. Twenty yards out, a lone coyote—his spirit animal—stood there looking at him, white-gold eyes glowing in the early morning light. They'd met a few weeks before, in the same place.

The two stared at each other for a long time before Otis tipped his tweed cap and closed his eyes again.

THE LOST ART OF CHASING DREAMS

Rory was standing in their Vermont kitchen, wearing one of his cheesy pinstriped suits. A red tie was pulled away from his neck, his typical after work appearance. With his politician's smile—the one Margot had grown to hate more than anything in the world—he asked, "What's for dinner?"

Margot raised her eyes at him from the cutting board, where a Santoku knife waited next to a pile of chopped garden carrots. "Hi, Sugar. So glad you're home." And with that, she took the knife by the blade and threw it at him with the expertise of a ninja. The blade embedded in his throat. She laughed, a sinister, devilish cackle, as he fell to his knees and bled to death on the kitchen floor, the last gurgles of his life a symphony of joy to her ears.

Margot Pierce reached for the glass of merlot she'd poured, sighing as she sank into the bubbles and savored the last moments of her daydream. Taking a bath in the early afternoon had become a ritual. So had imagining how she'd kill her ex-husband.

He had been the mayor of Burlington, Vermont, the father

of her only son, the man who tracked her down after seeing her in *Crazy for You* on Broadway in New York, put a ring on her finger, and dragged her back to Vermont. The man she'd left her promising career behind for: Rory Simpson. Just his name disgusted her now.

How unlucky she was to have been Margot Simpson, even temporarily. The name had invited an exhausting amount of teasing in comparison to the matriarch of *The Simpsons*. She'd changed her name back before he'd even signed the divorce papers. The bastard. The man whose affair was exposed by a journalist who managed to capture images of Rory's cock in his secretary's mouth—a slutty little whore named Nadine—a news story that made its rounds internationally and made Margot the most pitied woman in America.

These kinds of daydreams—admittedly disturbing as they were—had kept her from going insane since she left him. She attempted to keep each fantasized murder civil by only using objects found in the kitchen. It was the one rule to her cathartic game. One day, she'd have to quit killing him and move on to something else. It couldn't be healthy. Maybe she needed to see a therapist, but she didn't have time right now. She had a business to get off the ground, and things weren't off to the best start.

In a way, she had to appreciate his infidelity. Her half of his money had allowed her to move to Washington to realize her greatest dream: opening an inn and farm sanctuary. The inn was already being built, but the associated hemorrhaging of cash was starting to threaten the possibility of the farm sanctuary, a place where abused and neglected farm animals could live out their lives.

Since childhood, she'd been a protector of all living things, not even letting her friends squash a bug in her presence.

Philippe, her rescued three-year-old terrier mutt, was curled up on the cool tile floor against the wall. His wiry gray hair and royal gait made Margot think he belonged at the feet of Queen Guinevere while she held court. Margot spoiled him accordingly.

She'd bought her home and the land for the inn before she'd moved out to Red Mountain, but she couldn't yet purchase the adjoining ten acres for the sanctuary. At this rate, someone else might swoop in and buy the property out from under her. Every time she drove by, she wanted to grab the "For Sale" sign and put it in her trunk.

The inn was supposed to be open by now, but delays in construction had held up the project. Her contractor, a man she was learning to distrust, had assured her he'd be finished by September 1. Now, she'd be lucky to open the doors by June. And she'd be even luckier if she wasn't painfully over budget. *That's what I get for trusting someone, especially a man*, she thought. If her contractor wasn't careful, she'd be daydreaming about him in the bathtub, too. She had no shortage of kitchen weapons in her arsenal.

She dressed and went downstairs, Philippe following closely behind. Her home stood on the lower part of Red Mountain, below Col Solare, a winery owned by St. Michelle and the Antinori family. She'd bought the house from a Microsoft couple who'd built it only five years earlier. She never knew why they left, but the house was everything she ever wanted. It wasn't very big, but she didn't need much space for herself and her son. The white stucco and red roof, that Santa Barbara kind of look, fit so perfectly with the desert climate and the vines that ran in rows as far as you could see in every direction.

The Microsoft couple had done an exceptional job inside,

too, sparing no expense on fixtures, appliances, and the little details. Due to the escalating nature of real estate on Red Mountain and the seller's market they were in, Margot paid top dollar, but she believed in her purchase. Red Mountain was only beginning to show its potential. One day, people would compare the area to Yountville or Calistoga.

She heard a car door shut and walked out the front door. Her seventeen-year-old son, Jasper, was getting a backpack out of his car. The sight of him brought her so much joy. Though Jasper hated her to say it, he was the most adorable boy, or man, she'd ever seen. He was barely 5'8", weighed maybe 150 pounds, and had this baby face that made her want to gobble him up. He'd attempted to hide his youth by growing a beard, but the effort was so patchy that it somehow only enhanced the cute factor. He had exceptional taste in clothes and took great pride in his dress.

Today, he was wearing a pair of red John Fluevog brogue shoes with dark jeans and an ironed white button-down shirt. And he'd been the one to iron it! His brown hair was shaggy and he wore glasses with thick rims. She'd offered him LASIK but he had no interest. He liked looking sophisticated. His beat-up wool fedora rarely left his head. The whole look especially worked when he got on the bench behind the piano, which is where he had spent the majority of his life. He had this kind of budding-jazz-star look, "the mad scientist on the ivories," as one of the college recruiters trying to poach him had said.

Margot was learning more and more that the only person she could really trust in this world was Jasper. Somehow, despite all the crap she and her husband had put their son through—the media bullshit, the agonizing divorce, her own mental breakdown—her son was still solid as a rock. As long as he was in her life, everything was going to be all right.

He reached down and greeted Philippe.

"How was school, sweetheart?"

"Not bad. I'm figuring it out. By graduation, I'll be running the show." Jasper was generally very quiet, a great listener, but he was rarely short of words with her, even if sometimes sarcastic. He had put all the anger he felt toward his father into taking care of her. *What an amazing man,* Margot thought. That's right: man. He was a man now. Jasper was an old soul, always acting twice his age. Alas, because of this maturity, he had a hard time making friends, finding little in common with kids his age.

He approached her, put his hand on her shoulder, and gave her a peck on the cheek. "What's going on with you?"

"About to make *culurgiones*, your favorite."

"Can I help?"

"Don't you have homework?"

"Yeah, but it can wait."

"Wait a minute. So you want to help your boring old mom make dinner tonight? How did I get so lucky?"

"I enjoy making dinner with you. Especially Sardinian. I could use some comfort food."

"Why don't you take an hour and play the piano? I know you're dying to." Jasper had proved to be an exceptional classical and jazz pianist, and staff from Julliard, the Berklee College of Music, and the New England Conservatory, among others, had been bugging them for years. Half of their decision to come to Red Mountain was for Jasper; one of the top piano teachers in the country lived close by in Richland.

As Jasper started inside, Margot noticed someone had stuck a piece of paper to his back that read *I love boys.* She caught up to him and ripped it off. He didn't notice and kept moving. Did he really like his new school? Without his father as mayor, she was worried people would treat his strange side with a bit more teasing. She didn't want to baby him, though. He could take care of himself. At least, she'd keep telling herself that.

Before following him back inside, Margot took a minute to look at the inn, or what was to be her inn. Her contractor was on vacation, and he'd failed to line up work while he was gone, so the site on the other side of her property was a ghost town. Actually, the only signs of life were her five hens pecking and scratching diligently at a patch of dirt near the yet-to-be-working fountain in the front. The actual exterior of the inn, built of concrete block, was up, but they hadn't even started stuccoing yet. The only landscaping they'd done was the line of young black locust trees along the driveway and parking area.

She named the inn Épiphanie, homage to her mother's side of the family, who came from Carcassonne in the southwest of France, no doubt the roots of Margot's deep love for cooking and European cuisine. Épiphanie stood two stories high, with eight rooms upstairs for guests, each with a private balcony. The architecture matched the Spanish style of her home. Downstairs, there was a giant dining room, a commercial kitchen, a wine cellar, two bathrooms, and a large entryway that would feature a grand piano for Jasper to dazzle guests with when they entered. On a clear day, from any chair on the back patio, you could see the snowy top of Mount Adams off to the west.

Margot went in to finish dinner. Jasper was on the Steinway in the living room warming up. She'd always enjoyed his playing, even when he was stabbing out "Heart and Soul" when he was five. Now *and* then, she could listen to him for hours.

Today, he was teasing Debussy. She pulled out the piece of paper she'd ripped off his back and looked at it again. Her blood boiled. Youth could be so damn cruel.

ACKNOWLEDGMENTS

Thank you to my lovely wife, who has given me the exact opposite marriage from the one in this book.

To my selfless beta readers, I couldn't do it without you.

Thanks to Debra and Elizabeth at The Pro Book Editor and to my cover designer J.D. Smith.

And thanks to all of you who continue to support my imagination.

ABOUT BOO

Bestselling author Boo Walker initially tapped his creative muse as a songwriter and banjoist in Nashville before working his way west to Washington State, where he bought a gentleman's farm on the Yakima River. It was there amongst the grapevines and wine barrels that he fell in love with telling stories that now resonate with book clubs around the world. Rich with colorful characters and boundless soul, his novels will leave you with an open heart and a lifted spirit.

Always a wanderer, Boo currently lives in Cape Elizabeth, Maine with his wife and son. He also writes thrillers under the pen name Benjamin Blackmore. You can find him at boowalker.com and benjaminblackmore.com.

Made in the USA
Coppell, TX
27 August 2022

82098740R00111